"What Was Your Childhood Like?"

"Happy," Marc said, smiling. "Apparently the direct opposite of yours."

"Were you a paperboy?" Monica asked quickly. Now that she'd said too much, she wanted only to divert Marc's thoughts from her own life.

"Matter of fact, I was," he said. "And a Boy Scout, too."

"I bet you even helped little old ladies cross busy streets," she teased.

"I believe I did," he said with strange seriousness. "And ever since, I've had a soft spot for women in trouble."

Monica slowly lifted her eyes and met his gaze. The smile on her face faded. "Don't, Marc. Don't make the mistake of thinking I need you. I don't need anyone. I never have, and I never will."

"But you *do* need me, Monica," Marc said softly, amusement suddenly flickering in his eyes. "Or have you forgotten your—how shall I say it? Your predicament?"

Dear Reader:

Welcome! You hold in your hand a Silhouette Desire—your ticket to a whole new world of reading pleasure.

A Silhouette Desire is a sensuous, contemporary romance about passions, problems and the ultimate power of love. It is about today's woman—intelligent, successful, giving—but it is also the story of a romance between two people who are strong enough to follow their own individual paths, yet strong enough to compromise, as well.

These books are written by, for and about every woman that you are—wife, mother, sister, lover, daughter, career woman. A Silhouette Desire heroine must face the same challenges, achieve the same successes, in her story as you do in your own life.

The Silhouette reader is not afraid to enjoy herself. She knows when to take things seriously and when to indulge in a fantasy world. With six books a month, Silhouette Desire strives to meet her many moods, but each book is always a compelling love story.

Make a commitment to romance—go wild with Silhouette Desire!

Best,

Isabel Swift
Senior Editor & Editorial Coordinator

KATHERINE GRANGER
Unwedded Bliss

Silhouette Desire

Published by Silhouette Books New York

America's Publisher of Contemporary Romance

SILHOUETTE BOOKS
300 East 42nd St., New York, N.Y. 10017

Books by Katherine Granger

Silhouette Desire

Ruffled Feathers #392
Unwedded Bliss #410

KATHERINE GRANGER

had never read a romance until 1975, when a friend dumped a grocery bag filled with them in her living room and suggested she might enjoy them. Hooked with the very first one, Ms. Granger became a closet romance writer three years later. When she isn't writing, she teaches creative writing and composition at a community college and freshman composition at her alma mater. Katherine lives in Connecticut with her cat Barnaby. She enjoys movies, theater, golf, the Boston Red Sox, weekends at New England country inns and visits to Cape Cod.

For my mother,
with all my love

One

Monica Bliss had been listening to the ticking of her biological clock for the past two years. It was now time to do something about it. She adjusted the collar of her silk blouse, smoothed a slender hand over her tweed skirt, and took off her horn-rimmed glasses. Glancing in the mirror, she inspected the glossy platinum blond hair that framed her oval face, pinched a little color into her cheeks, then opened her office door.

"Mr. English," she said in her low, well-modulated voice, "won't you come in?"

She watched as Marc English unfolded his muscular six-foot four-inch frame from the Chippendale sofa in her reception area. He wasn't the type of man she liked. He was too dominant, too vitally masculine for her taste, but everything else about him fit her specifications—good looks, good breeding, good brain. She inspected him thoroughly as he walked into her office, taking in the breadth of his shoulders, the impeccable cut of his suit, the ironic arch of his brow.

"Are you ogling me, Monica?" he asked, a corner of his sensually sculpted mouth lifting in amusement.

"Certainly not!" She turned to her secretary. "Will you hold all calls, Terry?" The young woman nodded and Monica closed the door and faced him. "Won't you sit down?"

"If you don't mind," he said, "I'll stand." He shoved his hands in his trouser pockets. "What can I do for you?" His admiring glance slid up and down her trim figure, causing her to shiver unexpectedly.

She went to stand behind her desk. Somehow, she felt safer, less vulnerable that way. "I wish you'd sit down, Marc."

"Marc, is it?" he asked, chuckling softly. "You haven't called me Marc since that night two years ago when I made a pass at you and you slugged me."

She lifted her chin, but kept her voice even. "Marc, I have to talk to you. Won't you please sit down?"

He gestured to her chair. "After you."

When they had both taken their seats—she behind the impressive mahogany pedestal desk, he on the other side of it—she placed her glasses on the desktop and stared uncertainly at her perfectly manicured nails. "This isn't easy for me, Marc," she began, half expecting him to interrupt with a mocking comment. "We've known each other a long time now."

He nodded, steepling his fingers as he rested his elbows on the arms of the wing chair. He propped his chin on his fingertips and watched her with steady eyes. "Did you ask me here to tell me that?"

She hesitated. There was still time to back out; it wasn't too late. She inspected him carefully, looking for any sign that he wasn't the right choice. His hair was so dark it appeared black, yet she knew it was a deep burnished brown with reddish highlights that gleamed in the sun. He had a straight nose, well-shaped brows and a pleasantly square jaw, hinting at strength and determination in his character. His lower lip was nicely curved, his eyes gray, his skin seemed permanently tanned.

Mentally, she tallied the rest of his assets. He was perfectly respectable. He was rich—not that she needed money, she was well-off in her own right. He came from an excellent family, though she'd often wondered how the Englishes had spawned such a rogue. She suppressed a sigh. There was just no escaping it—he was the one.

"Marc," she said without preamble, "I want to have a baby." She was delighted to see his normal composure crack. He raised a brow and stared at her, openly startled.

"You *what*?"

"I want to have a baby."

By now he'd recovered. He thrust his long legs out and slid lower in the high-backed chair. "Is this your odd way of announcing your engagement?"

She smiled painfully. "No, it's my way of saying I'm thirty-five years old and I want a child. I have no intentions of marrying just to have one, so I have to come up with an alternative."

He was beginning to look wary. She felt her mouth tremble with a half smile. Good. She liked the idea of worrying Marc English—he'd once told her he knew her backward and forward, cover to cover, like a familiar book. He'd said she was predictable and boring. Let's just see how predictable and boring he thought she was now.

"What are you saying, Monica?"

"I've considered the few alternatives available to me. I won't marry a man just to have a child. I don't like the idea of a sperm bank; I wouldn't know who the donor was, and anyway, I want to be sure my child comes from good stock. There's no other way, really."

"No other way than what?" He was looking at her with half-closed eyes, his head tilted slightly back and to the side, the beginning of a smile on his mouth. She felt a sudden urge to run, but resisted.

"I need a man to have a baby with," she said. "And I've chosen you."

He was shaking his head admiringly, his silvery eyes glittering with amusement. "My Lord," he said, chuckling softly. "How like the ever-efficient Monica Bliss to announce it this way. I'm surprised you didn't say you needed a man to have sex with."

"Sex doesn't have anything to do with it," she said, trying to ignore the spasm in her heart. "You'd just have to go to the doctor's office and...um...make your contribution. I'd take care of the rest."

He stopped looking amused. "You'd have *my* child and—"

"No, Marc. It would be *my* child," she interrupted. "I'd ask you to sign an agreement to renounce all rights."

"You've got it all figured out, haven't you?"

She inclined her head in acknowledgement. "I've been thinking about this for quite some time, Marc. Naturally, I thought it through carefully. In fact, I've drawn up the document." She opened her middle desk drawer and took out a sheet of paper. "I imagine you'll need time to think this over. You can call me when you reach a decision."

"Why?"

She cocked her head, not sure she understood his question. "Why should you call me?"

"No. Why me?"

She looked away from those penetrating eyes. "Well," she said slowly, "I suppose because you're..." She gestured vaguely. "You're intelligent, you come from a good family. It's your genes, I suppose. If I'm going to have a child, I want it to have the best start in life it can. The Englishes are an old and respected family—I couldn't find a man more suitable to father my child."

His eyes had grown even more unreadable, but she detected something far back in those gray depths that gave her pause. What was he thinking, sitting there slouched comfortably in that wing chair, looking impeccable in his three-piece suit? She shrugged her momentary doubts away and said, "It wouldn't be any trouble for you. You could stop by my doctor's office some morning on your way to work."

He raised his brows. "You've got it all arranged, haven't you, Monica? Right down to the time I'd make the donation."

She felt two spots of color unexpectedly creep into her cheeks. For the first time, she felt the awkwardness of the situation. Her gaze fell from his. "Marc, I should think you'd be flattered."

"Oh, I am," he said. "Very flattered. The ice maiden, Monica Bliss, has consented to bear my child."

"Not your child," she said coolly. "Mine. That's part of the agreement."

"What will I get out of this?"

His question bothered her. Before asking him here, she'd worried about that very point, then decided to try it anyway. "Well, I . . ."

He nodded darkly. "Just as I thought. As usual, you've been thinking only of yourself."

"If you dislike me so much," she said hotly, "why did you spend so many years making passes at me?"

His eyes flickered with something she couldn't identify, then he smiled, looking entirely at ease and confident. "It was a pleasant game, Monica, that's all. Surely you didn't think it was more? You didn't perhaps think I harbored a crush for you?"

She felt her cheeks turn crimson. "Of course not," she said and pushed back her chair and stood, her shoulders squared, her back as straight as a soldier's. "Thank you for coming, Marc. I hope you'll give this some serious thought."

"What would you do if I refused?"

"I . . ." She faltered, her eyes falling from his. "I don't know."

He nodded grimly. "Well, why don't you spend the afternoon thinking about it? I'll call you when I've had some time to consider this."

"You're not refusing?" she asked, feeling hope burgeon within her. She knew if he didn't refuse point-blank, she had a chance.

"No, Monica, I'm not." He took the agreement from her. "I'll call you."

She watched as he walked out then sat down heavily in her chair. She took a shaky breath, suddenly feeling as if she'd run a marathon. Her heart was beating heavily against her breast. She put her head back against the soft leather of her chair and closed her eyes. He wouldn't refuse. He couldn't. He was the only man she knew she'd even consider having a child with.

Opening her eyes, she looked out the window. Dark green fir trees stood in stark contrast to the brilliant scarlet-and-orange sugar maples that graced the front yard. Overhead, the autumn sky was a chill slate gray, and already the streetlights were flickering on.

Sighing, she leaned forward and turned on the brass lamp that sat on the corner of her desk. Her eye was caught by a picture in a brass frame. Picking it up, she smiled sadly and smoothed her hand over it. Amy, aged seven, in love with the world, and loved totally by her parents. The child's face was as familiar as her own, a round, smiling countenance with laughing blue eyes and dimples, grinning into the camera, exposing a missing front tooth.

Monica felt the unexpected pang she always felt at the sight of that missing tooth, then she put the picture down and massaged her temples. It had been a stressful interview with Marc and she had a meeting to attend tonight. Rousing herself, she depressed the intercom button. "Terry?"

"Yes, Ms. Bliss?"

"I won't be staying late, after all. You can go now."

"Yes, Ms. Bliss. Thank you. Have a nice evening, ma'am."

Monica smiled. "Thank you, Terry. You, too."

She waited until her secretary had locked the front door, then put on her suit jacket, turned off the lights, and left through her private entrance. She walked slowly toward the silver Mercedes in her reserved spot. On a whim, she turned and looked at her office building. Situated in the middle of Farmington village, it was a handsome, rambling, gray-shingled house, with white shutters and flower-boxes at the windows. In the summer the window boxes were filled with geraniums, but now, in early October, the geraniums were gone, replaced by purple mums.

Monica inhaled the chilly air and lifted her eyes to the heavens where a thin sliver of moon already lit the darkening sky. Even if Marc said no, she told herself, she had a lot to be thankful for. She was a successful lawyer, running the practice she'd inherited from her father. She was the president of Connecticut Women in Law. She had a condominium in Farmington, a vacation cabin in Vermont and a gold American Express card.

Frowning, she turned back to her car. Still, success in business hadn't filled the hollow in her heart. She presented a good facade, of course, and no one suspected she had given up very much to get what she had today. She went to parties, or out to dinner, or to the health club, but for the past few years, she'd spent less time going out. She was usually too tired after a day at her job to answer the many social invitations she still received, and preferred having a meal in front of the fireplace in the winter, or on the deck in the summer.

She scoffed to herself as she pulled her car into the main street. They weren't really social invitations any longer; they were business invitations. In central Connecticut, it was well known that Monica Bliss was a career woman. She had a no-nonsense reputation which had earned her the respect of her peers, but it had stopped most men from calling to ask for a date long ago.

Even Marc English had given up on her. She tightened her hands on the steering wheel as she pulled out of her parking lot. He'd pestered her for years, flirting with her outrageously, and she had put him off by explaining that she was too busy getting her career off the ground to date anyone. But two years ago, at Christmas, she'd finally agreed to a date at the ballet.

She tried not to remember the glow that had seemed to surround them that night. For a few hours, she'd allowed herself to dream. Perhaps now, she'd thought, with her practice running smoothly and her reputation established, she could afford time to work on her personal life. But then Marc had brought her home, and her dream had shattered. He'd told her he realized she was all business, and then had startled her with an equally businesslike proposition. He'd said he wanted to sleep with her as if they were discussing the weather, and she had promptly hauled off and slugged him with her pocketbook. He'd had a black eye for a week—or so she'd heard—and she had gone into social hibernation.

Monica pulled into the driveway of her exclusive condominium, glancing up at the other sheltered townhouses with their skylights, angled cedar clapboards, and cantilevered decks. She had just enough time for a bath, then she'd dress for her eight o'clock meeting. Hurrying into the building, Monica tried to suppress the nervous flutters that attacked her midsection. He couldn't refuse her. He just couldn't.

Marc kept her waiting five days, then called her Friday afternoon just before five. "I'll meet you at Rubino's at eight tonight," he said when she answered the phone.

"Marc?"

"Who else? Don't tell me you have another potential donor waiting in the wings."

"Of course not," she said, exasperation simmering in her veins. "What have you decided?"

"I'll tell you tonight," he said.

"Marc! *Have* you decided?"

He sighed elaborately. "Persistent, aren't you?"

"Marc, will you?" she asked, ignoring his comment.

"I'll tell you tonight," he repeated. "Goodbye, Monica."

Monica hung up, trying to still the clamor of her pulse. She'd find out tonight. She put a trembling hand to her lips. Please, she prayed, please let him say yes.

Rubino's was her favorite restaurant, a dimly lit place with deep carpets that hushed all noise, and lush green plants that created intimate dining pockets. Had Marc chosen it because he'd somehow found out she liked it, or because it would afford them the privacy they needed for their talk? As the maître d' led her to Marc's table, she laughed at herself. Marc had chosen it for the privacy. He was too contemptuous of her feelings to care whether she liked it or not.

When she arrived at the table, Marc stood up, and for just a moment, she wondered if she were wrong. He was acting the proper suitor. Maybe his polite behavior wasn't just for the benefit of the maître d', who'd already hurried away.

Two years ago, had there just been a massive communica-
tion problem between them? Had Marc treated an affair
with her like a business agreement because he assumed that's
how she would want it? She shook off her questions. It was
hardly the time to be thinking about the past. What had
happened was over. Now, she would only think of the future.

"Have you decided?" she asked the moment they were
seated.

He began to chuckle. "Always right down to business. If
I remember correctly, I tried that once and had quite a colorful complexion for a few days."

She sat back, acknowledging his point with a chagrined
smile. "You're right, of course. I'm sorry. It's just that I'm
so . . ." She looked at him, her blue eyes filled with anxiety.
Then she shook her head. "Forgive me. I suppose we should
have a pleasant dinner, then you can tell me." She tried to
ignore the shiver that went up her spine as his gaze flickered over her. She'd taken great pains with her appearance
and was dressed in black silk and spiked heels. She wore
pearls at her throat and a black coat with a black fox collar, which cradled her face in lustrous fur.

She slid off the coat and draped it over the back of her
chair, then propped her elbows on the table, resting her chin
on her folded hands. "I'd like a vodka martini—very dry."

Marc signaled a waiter. When he'd given her order, Marc
sat back and looked her up and down. "You're still the most
incredibly beautiful woman I know. What a shame you care
only about your work."

She looked down, masking her eyes with her long lashes.
"Why is it that men who care only for their work always
dislike women who do the same?"

He smiled thoughtfully. "Is that what you think about
me? That I'm a workaholic?"

She paused before answering, studying his face. What did she know about Marc English? He was also a lawyer, a prosecutor in the Chief State Attorney's office. Where she specialized in divorce and real-estate law, Marc was a criminal lawyer. She saw him occasionally on television, interviewed after various infamous court cases. She knew he worked long hours, but that was about all she knew. He kept his personal life private. His family was wealthy and well-known, but Marc had little to do with social affairs.

"I suppose I assumed work is your main concern," she said quietly, taking a sip of the martini that had appeared as if by magic.

"You're guilty of gross overgeneralization," he said, softening his words with a smile. "Just because your work is your whole life, you think everyone else is that way."

"And you're not?"

"Not at all. I work hard, Monica, but I have plenty of other interests."

"Such as?"

He took a moment to consider, then said, "Chess. I play a mean game of chess."

"I used to play with my father, but I haven't had a game in years."

"Really?" He studied her with amused eyes. "We'll have to have a match sometime."

Oddly, she felt as if they were engaged in one now. She plucked nervously at the linen napkin in her lap. "Marc, I can't sit here all evening without knowing. You've got to tell me what you've decided."

"That's just it. I haven't decided, Monica."

"You haven't.... But you said you'd tell me tonight."

"I will, after we talk." He tilted his head and considered her gravely. "If I were to help you have a child, Monica, I'd want to know I was doing the right thing."

She stared at him, then dropped her gaze. "I see. And what would convince you?"

"Honest answers to my questions."

She nodded, playing with the corner of the plush napkin. "Well, perhaps you'd better start asking them."

"You see that I have a right to ask certain questions, don't you?"

She hesitated, struggling with her response. Finally she nodded. "Yes. I understand that. If you asked me to carry a child for you, I'd want to know why you wanted a child before I undertook such a major change in my life." She lifted her clear blue eyes and met his gaze squarely. "Of course, it would be different for me, wouldn't it? I mean, all you have to do is . . ." She blushed, her cheeks turning a becoming pink. "Well, I mean, it's the woman who bears the burden of having a child, isn't it? The man simply . . ."

"Begins the process," he said softly, supplying a euphemism she'd been too embarrassed to find.

She nodded gratefully. "Yes, exactly."

"Why, Monica?" he asked now. "Why do you want a child so much?"

She shifted uncomfortably in her chair. How much could she tell him? Not everything, that was sure. To protect herself, she'd have to lie a little. But they would only be small lies, and very white ones. "What I told you in my office the other day is true, Marc. I'm thirty-five years old, and I want to have a baby. I want to experience carrying a child, and childbirth itself, and then . . ." She broke off, staring unseeingly at the tabletop. Slowly, her face relaxed.

"I want to hear a baby in my home, Marc," she said softly. "I want to hear my child laughing and gurgling, even crying. I want to smell her skin just after her bath, and the baby powder . . ." Her eyes grew luminous, and her face even more tender, revealing a vulnerability she seldom showed to anyone. "I want a house filled with little pink booties and little bibs and overalls and I want most of all to *hold* her, Marc, to watch her grow up and give her all the love she'll need, and—'' She broke off, embarrassed at her show of emotion. "Well," she said, laughing self-consciously. "You get the picture."

"Yes," he said softly, "I believe I do."

She looked up at the tone of his voice, and was startled to see understanding and compassion in his face. For some reason, that embarrassed her even more. "The biological clock is real, Marc," she said. "When I was younger, I thought I could do without a child in my life. Now, I know I can't." She searched his eyes. "Can you understand that?"

He looked at her thoughtfully, then nodded slowly. "Yes, I can understand it, Monica."

"You'll do it, then?" she asked, leaning forward eagerly.

He didn't answer right away, but sat playing with his silverware. Then he lifted solemn eyes and said, "Yes, but only under one condition."

She heard only the words she wanted to hear. Elation bubbled through her. "Oh, Marc," she breathed, eyes shining. "I'm so happy—"

"Perhaps you didn't hear me," he interrupted gently. "I said I'd do it under one condition."

She sat back, trying to keep her joy under control. Tears misted her eyes. "All right," she said softly. "What is it, Marc?"

"That we do it the old-fashioned way," he said dryly. "Together. In a bed preferably, for as long as it takes."

Two

She stared at him, stunned. "I don't understand."

His eyes gleamed with amusement. "Oh, I'm sure you understand very well," he said. "I'm perfectly willing to help you have a child, Monica, and I'll even sign that silly paper you drew up, but I'm not going to do it by making a deposit in some anonymous sperm bank. If I do it at all, it will be as I said—the old-fashioned way." He tilted his head and considered her. "Does that upset you?"

She put all the ice she could muster into her voice. "The only thing that upsets me is the way this surprised me. I should have known you'd come up with a dirty angle on this."

"Dirty?" The amusement left his face. "I don't see it as dirty, Monica." He studied her. "Do you think women are the only ones who want to experience intimacy and warmth?"

"What do you mean?"

"Let's just say I don't like the idea of children conceived in test tubes." He shook his head, his eyes clouded. "There's something unnatural about depositing sperm in a jar and having a doctor implant it. The world is impersonal enough. Must we dehumanize creation, too?" He paused, as if considering his words carefully. "You said the biological clock is real. Well, my time's running out, too."

"But it's different for men," she said. "You could father a child when you're fifty. Why, even men in their sixties and seventies father children."

"Father them, yes, but are they around to watch them grow up? Perhaps it *is* different for men, but I don't think it's substantially different. I'm forty-one years old, Monica, and I've never married, but I haven't stayed single because I wanted to. I simply haven't found a woman I cared enough about to want to marry."

She stared at him, suddenly apprehensive. She didn't want a man to marry her, she just wanted a baby. "Marc, you said you'd sign that agreement. You wouldn't have any rights to my child."

He nodded grimly. "That's right. I'm willing to do that, but I'd know she was mine, and that would make all the difference. I wouldn't make trouble for you after she was born. When I asked you why you wanted a child, it was to find out if you'd make a suitable mother. I think you would, Monica. It surprises the hell out of me, but I think you would. When you were talking about having a baby, you showed a part of yourself I didn't know existed. So, yes, I'm willing to do it, but it has to be my way."

She uneasily drew circles on the tablecloth. If he ever found out the truth, would he still feel she'd make a suitable mother? She had to steer clear of any personal involvement; it might prove fatal to her plan. "There's one thing I don't understand," she said finally. "I can understand your desire to have a child. I can even accept that you'd be willing to give her up and watch her from afar, but . . ." She trailed off, unable to put her thoughts into words.

"You can't understand why I want to sleep with you to do it, is that it?" he asked.

"Exactly."

He frowned thoughtfully, then tilted his head, as if assessing the impact his words would have. "I find you very attractive, Monica. I've wanted to sleep with you for years. So, there we have it—you want something from me, and I want something from you, and for the strangest of reasons, we both find ourselves in a position to give each other what we most want." He arched a brow over amused eyes. "How about it? It seems eminently fair to me."

She was so angry she found herself shaking. "That whole song and dance about time running out was just a joke to you, wasn't it?" she asked in a low voice that trembled with suppressed emotion. "That was a convenient excuse you thought might work. When it didn't, you resorted to the truth."

He shrugged. "Think what you want. I'd just like you to consider *my* offer." He picked up his menu, as if to signal the end of that part of the conversation. "Have you tried the veal piccata here?"

"But—"

He glanced up at her. "Yes?"

Her earlier joy had drained away completely. "Nothing."

He sat considering her, then put the menu down and took her hand. The gesture startled her, but no more than what he said. "Monica, a child should be conceived in love. Barring that, maybe the next best thing is for two people who respect each other to have a child. I *know* what matters is that the child be loved and wanted. I can give you a child, Monica, but I refuse to do it as if it were nothing but a stop at the neighborhood drugstore. If we can't conceive a child in love, Monica, at least we can do it in a way that isn't cold and antiseptic.''

He reached out and brushed a lock of hair back from her cheek. The warmth of his hand and lightness of his touch surprised her, making her heart race painfully. ''Think about it, Monica. We might grow to like each other. Maybe we'd even learn to care for each other. Wouldn't you want that for your child, Monica? To know that her parents at least made love with the loving object of giving her life?''

Monica lifted confused eyes and stared into his face. There was tenderness there, and concern, even compassion. She struggled with the knowledge that he had a point, yet she wasn't ready to make such a major decision. She felt a sudden surge of panic rise up in her. If she stayed here for even another moment she might scream, or faint, or make some sort of public spectacle of herself. ''I'll call you, Marc,'' she said, pulling on her coat.

He raised his eyebrows questioningly. ''You mean you won't stay for dinner?'' If she didn't know better, she'd almost think he was disappointed.

''No, Marc, I . . . I just can't.'' She met his eyes and for a moment she regretted her decision. He actually looked hurt, but she must be mistaken. Shoving her chair back, she stood up and hurried from the restaurant, surprised to find herself shaking.

She couldn't do it. It was impossible. The idea of cold-bloodedly getting into bed with a man to conceive a child, even if the man were as attractive as Marc English, was reprehensible to her. She was as red-blooded as the next woman, but she also had standards. She'd made love with only one man in her life, and she'd thought she loved him. She couldn't imagine agreeing to Marc's outrageous demand.

And anyway, she had to steer clear of getting involved with him. If he ever found out about her secret, he might take her to court, claiming she was an unfit mother.

Monica groaned and put her head in her hands, resting her elbows on her desktop. She hadn't accomplished a thing all weekend, and here it was Monday afternoon and she hadn't gotten any work done today, either. Her eyes wandered to the photograph of Amy. As she sat and stared at it, the old gnawing hunger welled up again. Dammit, she was a woman and yet she hadn't been able to enjoy one of woman's greatest joys—her own child.

Rubbing her forehead, she swung her chair around and looked unseeingly out the window. Dusk was falling rapidly. She'd sent her secretary home already, and was alone here, unable to come to a decision. Or rather, she thought she knew what she'd decided, but couldn't bring herself to call Marc and tell him. That would make it final. If she called and told him no, all her dreams would go down the drain.

"You can't have everything your own way, you know, Monica Marie." Her father's stern voice came back to her, as clear as if he were standing in the room with her. She closed her eyes and visualized him—tall and silver haired and exceptionally handsome, a debonair man who had amassed a fortune by hard work. He'd never gotten over the disappointment that his only child was a girl. She had done everything possible to make up for it—she'd studied hard and been the top student in her classes all the way through law school.

She swiveled her chair around and looked at the phone. She had given up everything she'd ever wanted to please her father. She'd loved him fiercely, aching for his love in return, yet he'd died three years ago without ever once having told her he loved her.

Reaching out, she picked up the phone and punched Marc's number, then sat listening to the ring. She was about to hang up when a brusque voice growled "Hello."

"Marc?"

"Nah, he ain't here. This is Smitty."

Monica smiled to herself. How could she ever have confused the elegant Marc English with short, squat, balding Oliver Smith, otherwise known as Smitty? "Hello, Smitty," she said, sitting back. "This is Monica."

"Monica Schmonica. I know a million Monicas. How the hell you expect me to know who—?" He broke off, and she could imagine his face as it lit up in a hundred-watt grin. "Monica Bliss? How you doin'?"

"I'm fine, Smitty. How're you? Still knee-deep in larceny?"

"Ya know, Monica, I swear the criminal element's takin' over the world. Just yesterday, I spent five hours in court, only to have the bum get off on a technicality. I tell you, you were smart goin' into divorce."

"Hey, I tried to tell you back in law school..."

"I know, I know, but can you see me in a swank West Hartford divorce case? Me, five-one and two hundred pounds? And speakin' like this?"

"Oh, Smitty," she said, laughing softly. "You're still the same."

"You expect me to change?" He snorted. "Hell'll freeze first." Then his voice changed. "But how're you? I never see you. You doin' okay?"

"I'm doing fine, Smitty." She glanced at her watch and her smile fled. "You don't know where Marc is by any chance, do you?"

"Marc English?"

"Is there another Marc?" she asked dryly.

"No, but last I heard, you and him were on the outs."

"Oh? What'd you hear?"

"I heard you decked him, couple years ago Christmas."
Monica groaned. "He told you that?"

"Yeah. Said you was mad as a hornet." Smitty chuckled. "He had a shiner for a week." She could hear him twist in his chair, probably getting more comfortable. "So, Monica, what you callin' Marc for? Wanna get in a little target practice?" He broke up laughing and Monica waited for him to stop, tapping her toe irritably.

"Smitty, you're as obnoxious as you were in school. It's a wonder anyone even talks to you."

"Yeah, I know," he said, then began laughing again.

"Goodbye, Smitty," she said sternly.

"Bye, Monica. Good talkin'."

She hung up, then lowered her head to her hands. If Marc had told Smitty what happened two years ago, everyone in the world knew. Smitty had a megaphone for vocal chords. Then, hesitantly, her lips began to tremble in a smile, until finally she couldn't stop herself from laughing out loud. How like Marc to tell the world, and how like Smitty to report on it.

"Are you sitting in here laughing all alone, Monica?"

Startled, she raised her head, her eyes wide, a hand at her throat. "Marc!"

He was leaning against the door holding a bouquet of red roses, a trench coat slung over his shoulder. "You should lock your door when your secretary leaves. Anyone could walk in here."

"Anyone just did," she said dryly.

The corner of his mouth twitched in amusement, then he held out the flowers. "They cost me an arm and a leg, but nothing's too good for the mother of my child."

"You know what they say about people who assume too much."

He grinned, slinging his trench coat over a chair. "Don't tell me you're going to chicken out, Monica."

She took the flowers and buried her nose in them, a ruse to give herself time to formulate an answer, but the faint scent of the roses tantalized her, chasing away all coherent thought. When she peeled off the tissue-paper wrapping, the aroma of roses enveloped her. Taking a shaky breath, she stood up and began stripping the lower leaves off the long stems.

"Do you like them?" Marc asked.

She raised her eyes to his. "I love them."

They stood looking into each other's eyes, then she pulled herself away and hurried into the lavatory to fill a vase with water. She was damned if she was going to let a rogue like Marc English sweet-talk her. When she'd arranged the flowers, she knew she couldn't put off the inevitable any longer. She closed the office door, then leaned back against it. "I just called your office," she said. "I talked with Smitty a while."

"Yeah," he said, nodding. "I heard you."

For some reason, she wasn't surprised that he'd been listening in the reception area. She pushed away from the door and began tidying the magazines that were scattered on the coffee table in front of the couch. "Why are you here, Marc?" she finally asked.

"I was just driving by and thought I'd drop in," he said nonchalantly, then added. "But I also want to know your answer."

She felt her stomach churn with anxiety. Straightening, she turned away, folding her arms tightly as she stared at the Mary Cassatt painting of a mother and child over the mantel. Her father had bought it for her when she graduated from law school. Remembering that time, she felt her throat close up with sudden emotion, but she forced herself to speak. "I'm sorry to disappoint you, Marc, but the answer is no."

When he didn't respond, she turned around slowly. He was leaning against her desk, his head tilted to one side, his eyes narrowed as he studied her. "Why?"

Shrugging, she made a nervous gesture, then regretted revealing her nervousness. "I suppose it's silly, really, this being the twentieth century and all, but I..." She fiddled with an errant lock of hair, frowning. "Somehow it seems more difficult your way. I mean, my way was cleaner, simpler. There was no involvement. It just seemed—" She looked back at him, and felt her heart stop.

He was holding the picture of Amy, studying it. Slowly, he raised his head and looked at her, then put the picture down. "Go on." he said. "It seemed what?"

She took a steadying breath and inconspicuously wiped her palms on her skirt. "It seemed more difficult, that's all."

"Why?" He had folded his arms and was waiting patiently. She almost smiled. He was the picture of the perfect courtroom lawyer—cool, deliberative, resolutely waiting for the defendant to make a mistake.

"Marc..." She shrugged helplessly. "I can't just sleep with a man. I mean, there has to be some feeling involved."

"You wouldn't be sleeping with just any man," he said reasonably. "You'd be sleeping with the man you've chosen to father your child."

"Marc, I can't just go to bed with you."

"Why not? Are you a virgin?"

She shook her head at him, almost amused. "No."

"Then what's the problem? You can't think I've got some social disease or you wouldn't have talked to me in the first place."

"I..." She lifted her chin proudly. "I've never slept with a man I didn't love, Marc. I can't just go to bed with you and..."

"Make love?"

She frowned. "That's just it. It wouldn't be making love. It would be having sex."

He levered himself away from her desk, shoved his hands in his pockets, and began to wander the room, his head down, his expression thoughtful. Finally, he lifted his head and looked at her. "You think it would be that bad, huh?"

She almost laughed. "It would be *awkward*, dammit!"

"So you'd give up your dream of having a child because you might feel awkward at first?"

She studied him. "I was hoping I wouldn't have to give up my dream, Marc," she said. "I was hoping you'd change your mind."

"I see. So we're back at square one."

She met his gaze evenly, but for some reason, she felt uncomfortable. Turning, she looked up at the painting. It was strange that she kept it despite how much she hated it. But she somehow felt that selling it would be like turning her back on the past. She shook off the memories and turned to look at Marc. He was leaning against the desk again, his eyes unreadable. She'd never seen eyes quite like his before. If she allowed herself, she thought absently, she'd almost find the man attractive....

"Come here, Monica," he said softly. "I have a proposition for you."

She felt her heart skip a beat, then settle back into place. "What do you mean?"

"I mean come here," he repeated in a low voice.

She stared at him, recognizing the seductive tone in his voice. What did he think he was going to do? Seduce her into bed with him? She smiled to herself and walked slowly toward him. "Well," she said, her husky voice threaded with amusement, "what do you want?"

"A week of your time."

She searched his eyes, feeling a knot uncurl in her stomach. "I don't understand."

"Give me a week to convince you," he said.

"Convince me of what?"

His eyes traveled a lazy path to her lips, then lifted to hers. "That it wouldn't be so awkward."

She stared at him, feeling a sudden surge of awareness spiral deliciously up her spine. She shook it off, amazed at the conceit of the man. "The answer is no, Marc. N-O."

He lay his finger lightly against her lips. "Shhh," he whispered. "Don't say something you really don't mean."

She stared into his eyes and felt something strange happen. The room began to swirl, or perhaps it was just her stomach. And there was this delicious warmth seeping into her bones. How very disconcerting to have her knees go weak at a time like this, right when she needed to be her strongest.

She drew away and lifted her chin defiantly. "You really are the most egotistical man I know," she said. "Do you honestly think you could do anything to change my mind in just a week?"

The corner of his mouth twitched, but he didn't answer right away. Instead, he took her hand and began to examine it slowly, turning it over to explore her palm, tracing the lines with a light touch that sent shivers across her sensitive skin. "Yes," he said finally, lifting his eyes to hers, "I honestly think I could."

She pulled her hand from his grasp. "I'm sorry," she said coolly, "but you're wrong. Now if you'll excuse me, I have work to do." She turned away, but his next words stopped her.

"Just give me a week, Monica," Marc said. "At the end of the week, if you still want it your way, we'll do it your way."

Slowly she turned to face him. "What did you say?"

"You heard me," he said, his eyes gleaming with amusement. "I think it's a fair deal. If you're still not comfortable enough to sleep with me by a week from today, I'll do things your way. But it would only be sporting of you to give me a chance to get what I want, too."

She had to admire his persistence. She liked a man who didn't give up too easily—even if this particular man had an ego ten times too large for his own good. Not that she would change her mind. She could spend a month in his company and not want to sleep with him. She didn't like men who came on strong. She'd had a lifetime of being dominated by her father. She preferred a man who was tender rather than insensitive, who respected her wishes rather than riding roughshod over them.

The one suitor in her life had been quiet, gentle, and kind. She frowned to herself, shaking off the suspicion that she'd attributed strengths to him, rather than weaknesses. One thing was certain, Marc English would never be able to overcome her dislike in seven days. All she had to do was hold out for a week and she'd get what she wanted. It would be as easy as sliding on ice.

"All right," she said. "You've got yourself a deal."

He held up a warning hand. "Let's agree on the ground rules first."

She rested against her desk. "The ground rules," she repeated, smiling. "All right. What have you got in mind?"

"You've got to give us a chance, Monica. That means spending some time with me."

She arched a wry brow. "What do you expect? That I devote an entire week to you?"

"Only the evenings." She was about to protest, but he held up a hand. "Hear me out, Monica. If we're going to get to know each other, we'll need to spend some time together. It wouldn't be a true test if you didn't agree to that up front."

Monica tapped a polished fingertip on her desk. "Are we talking every night?"

He nodded, folding his arms and leaning back against the wall. "Every night and all weekend."

"All—"

"Now, Monica," he said, interrupting before she could say another word. "Those are my ground rules."

"The evenings are no problem, but I'd planned to go to Vermont this weekend."

He shrugged. "So? I'll go with you."

She stared at him, trying to envision smooth, cosmopolitan Marc English in the backwoods of Vermont seeking out antiques. The very idea brought a smile to her lips. "I'm going antiquing," she said softly. "You'd hate it."

"I tell you what," he said. "We'll compromise. If you agree to spend tonight and the next three nights doing whatever I want, I'll agree to spend the weekend in Vermont doing whatever you want."

She began to laugh softly. "You'll never make it."

"Try me," he murmured.

She tilted her head and considered him. How would he look out of those expensive, hand-tailored suits of his? She couldn't see him in worn jeans or corduroys; he was too much of a fashion plate. She almost laughed out loud at the picture of Marc without his silk ties and starched shirts.

Suddenly she went still, envisioning him without his shirt, seeing swirls of dark hair rising in a cloud from a powerfully muscled chest. The picture was so real she felt heat sweep over her, felt her heartbeat begin to accelerate. Swallowing awkwardly, she shook off the image.

"My weekend place isn't exactly luxurious, Marc," she warned him. "It's a little log cabin out in the boondocks. The only company for miles are owls and field mice."

"Does it have indoor plumbing?"

She smiled slowly, beginning to like this scheme after all. "Yes, but that's about the only modern convenience. I heat it with a wood stove and fireplace, and the hot water heater is notoriously undependable."

He shrugged. "I'll just have to put up with it then."

"Yes," she said, her blue eyes gleaming. "I guess you will."

"Then you agree with the ground rules?"

She hesitated, then nodded. "I agree."

He relaxed into a grin. "Good." He looked at his watch. "How about dinner?"

Her first impulse was to refuse, then she realized she'd just agreed to spend tonight and the next three nights doing whatever he wanted. She told herself it was a small price to pay to fulfill a dream. She stifled her objection and nodded. "All right."

"Rubino's?" he asked.

Telling herself she had nothing to worry about, she nodded. "Rubino's would be fine."

Three

Rubino's was quiet on this Monday evening. Classical music played in the background, punctuated by the muted laughter of the few other customers, the tinkle of ice in fine crystal, and the clink of sterling silver against bone china. Salmon-colored lilies in cut-glass bowls graced each table, and candles flickered behind glass hurricane shades.

Monica slid gracefully into the chair held by Marc, then eyed him sardonically as he took a seat across from her and ordered drinks. "It won't work, Marc," she said. "You can bring me to the nicest restaurant in Hartford, you can wine and dine me and play the perfect gentleman, but you're not going to convince me to go to bed with you."

"I'm not trying to convince you to go to bed with me," he said reasonably. "I'm only trying to give us enough time together so you'd see it wouldn't necessarily be awkward if we did."

"You make it all seem so gallant," she said ironically, "as if this is some sort of humanitarian campaign you're waging."

He tilted his head considerably. "Maybe it is, in a way. Maybe it wouldn't be such a bad gift to mankind to help you get over your aversion to men."

"I'm not averse to men, Marc," she said tartly. "I'm only averse to *you*."

He shook his head, his eyes filled with mocking laughter. "As they say in Washington, it won't wash, Monica. It doesn't make sense. If you dislike me so much, why did you choose me to father your child?"

She almost had to look away from those knowing eyes, but the taunting look in them put steel in her backbone. "It has nothing to do with *you*," she said pointedly, "and everything to do with your pedigree."

"My pedigree," he said, nodding thoughtfully. "I see."

"Yes, your pedigree. Like it or not, I have to admit you come from good stock, but don't be smug about it."

"I'm not smug, Monica," he said quietly. "I'm anything but smug." For some reason, he wasn't laughing any more.

Startled by his reaction, she stared at him, seeing something that looked almost like vulnerability in his face. She sat back, unprepared for his response. For a moment, she'd been tempted to reach out and comfort him. Now, wasn't that absurd. "Don't use that puppy-dog appeal on me, Buster," she warned ironically. "I'm not buying."

"Puppy-dog appeal?" he repeated blankly.

"That hangdog look, that hand-on-the-heart, woe-is-me, *humble* approach." She mimicked him, "'I'm not smug, Monica. I'm anything but smug.'"

He burst out laughing. "You're really good. Can you do Humphrey Bogart?"

The absurdity of his question caught her off guard and she began to giggle. "No, but I do a great Mae West."

"Why, Monica Bliss," Marc said, his voice curiously warm, "This is a whole other side of you I didn't know existed. Mae West." He shook his head disbelievingly. "Do her."

"Oh, Marc...."

"Come on, Monica. Just once."

It was totally ridiculous. A respected attorney didn't sit in the plushest restaurant in Hartford and do imitations of Mae West. It just wasn't done. Then she shrugged and leaned forward anyway, arching a brow seductively, "Why doncha come up and see me sometime?" she purred.

Marc put back his head and roared with laughter, and suddenly she was joining him, a hand to her mouth, trying desperately to stem the laughter that wouldn't be contained. "Oh, this is too embarrassing," she said between gasps of laughter. "Oh, Lord, what will people think?" She laughed even harder then, shrugging carelessly. "Who cares what they think?"

Marc's laughter gradually died out until he was just smiling at her, his eyes filled with admiration. "I like you like this, Monica Bliss."

She felt a curious warmth invade her, and suddenly she had to look away. There was something almost scary about the look in Marc's eyes, as if he truly *did* like her. She lifted her chin in mock hauteur. "I can let down my hair," she said. "I just don't do it very often."

"Well, you should," Marc said. "It's very becoming."

His compliments were real, she realized, and suddenly her playful mood disappeared, as quickly as it had come. "That's the only thing I dislike about being a lawyer—there's no time to play. Everything is work, work, work."

"You run your own practice," he said. "Why not cut down on the work load?"

"I suppose I could, but everyone else I know is working as hard as I am, even my friends who aren't career women." Her brow knitted into frown lines. "Do you ever get the feeling the world is going too fast, Marc?"

"All the time. I don't know if it's just old age creeping up, but time seems suddenly to be fastened to a runaway train, and I'm just hanging on desperately for the ride."

She smiled and sipped the drink the waiter placed in front of her. "I don't think it's old age. I think it's the world. Everyone says the same thing. We're all hurrying and no one seems to know where we're hurrying to." She traced a line on the plush linen tablecloth and found herself confessing something she rarely even admitted to herself. "Sometimes I wish I could just walk into a Norman Rockwell painting, like a *Twilight Zone* story. You know, just walk into it and be in that world, where everything is slower and more peaceful."

"Why, Monica Bliss," Marc said gently, "you are surprising the daylights out of me."

She leaned her elbows on the table and rested her chin on her folded hands. "What did you think I was like?" she asked, smiling drowsily. "All chain metal and rawhide, with a clock for a heart?"

"No..." he said slowly, sitting back and smiling in return. "I always wondered if there were a softer side, a part of you that wasn't all business, but you never showed it to me, or to anyone else for that matter. Your reputation is all-business." He hesitated a moment, then said, "That's why I came on to you the way I did two years ago."

She dropped her gaze from his and shifted uncomfortably in her chair. "I see...." They'd been doing so well. Why did he have to bring up that old scene? She fiddled with her drink stirrer. "I *was* hurt, Marc."

"Yes," he said quietly. "I know. I was so damned angry at myself. I've wanted to apologize for two years now, but I

couldn't bring myself to do it. I felt like a complete fool.
You were right to slug me. I deserved it."

She lifted her eyes, astonished at his apology. She
searched his face, looking for evidence that he was putting
her on, but she couldn't find it. She smiled and shrugged.
"It's in the past now."

"Do you forgive me?"

She hesitated. Did she? "I'm not sure if I do or not," she
said slowly. She looked at him speculatively. "I'm not sure
what I feel about you, Marc English."

"Well," he said, "you've got a week to find out."

Yes, she thought, an entire week. If nothing else, it would
probably prove interesting....

At her front door two hours later, Marc stood a good
three feet away from her, his hands shoved in his trouser
pockets. "I'll pick you up tomorrow about seven," he said.
"Will that give you enough time to get ready?"

"Where are we going?" she asked. Frankly, she was surprised he wasn't trying to kiss her good-night. If he were
bent on seducing her, he sure was hiding it well.

"Oh, right. You would want to know that, wouldn't
you?"

"It would help," she said gently. "I do dress differently
if I'm bowling or going to the theater."

"I have tickets for the symphony tomorrow night at the
Bushnell, and for Hartford Stage Wednesday night, if that's
okay with you."

"My goodness," she said, smiling. "You believe in
showing a woman a good time, don't you?"

"Nothing but the best, Monica," he said, grinning.
"Prime time all the way."

"What about Thursday night?"

He looked her straight in the eye, and for some reason, his words seemed to carry extra freight. "We'll find something to do, I'm sure."

She felt her pulse jump erratically. Drawing herself up to her full height, she put a little discouraging chill in her words. "Yes, well..." She smiled her most formal smile. "Good night, Marc. I'll see you at seven tomorrow."

He smiled knowingly, as if to say that he could see through her little ruse. "Good night, Monica," he said, and turned and walked away.

She found his knowing little smile strangely irritating. But the fact that he walked away and didn't even try to kiss her was, ironically, even more so.

On the Bushnell stage, the Hartford Symphony was warming up, making all those discordant noises an orchestra always makes in preparation. The audience was slowly filling up the auditorium, but Monica was only conscious of Marc's broad shoulder that brushed against hers and his muscular thigh that seemed to touch hers more than absolutely necessary. They had aisle seats, and to Monica, it seemed that the entire audience was entering by way of their row. She and Marc had to stand and let people by, or scrunch up and let them pass, and every time, Marc put a solicitous arm around her, as if protecting her from possible harm.

To make matters worse, he was wearing cologne that was extraordinarily provocative, and he looked fantastic dressed in a dark suit and white shirt that set off his perpetually tanned face. If she didn't know he was the son of Elliot Walsh English, she would have sworn Marc was Italian.

"How do you do it?" she asked, leaning to whisper in his ear.

"How do I do what?" He turned to look at her and she found herself uncomfortably close to him.

For a moment she couldn't speak, she could only stare into his eyes and listen to the absurd tom-tom that had taken residence in her heart. Immediately, she pulled herself together. "How do you stay tan all year long?"

"I'm not," he said. "I'm just naturally dark."

She gave him a knowing look. "I remember watching your mother from a distance years ago. She had skin like porcelain, and your father has sandy red hair and a complexion that's as florid as they come. Why don't you just admit it? You go to one of those ridiculous tanning salons."

He shrugged. "Whatever you say, Monica."

"What's it like lying in a little box and being baked by alpha rays, or whatever they are?"

"I'm sure it's properly hedonistic," he said, browsing through the program.

She was about to respond, but the conductor walked out on stage and the audience erupted into applause. But though the music crashed around her, she remained excruciatingly aware of Marc. His shoulder seemed to loom larger than Gibraltar's Rock. His cologne scented the air. His presence was all encompassing, permeating the surroundings until the magnificent soar of the violins, the triumphant cry of the horns, the booming crash of the cymbals were all reduced to insignificant background music. Marc had her complete attention and every cell in her body seemed attuned to his presence.

Then she realized he was watching her. She turned her head slowly and met his gaze and couldn't look away. They sat looking at each other, vividly attuned in the darkened concert hall, until finally she had to pull her eyes off him, turning her head to gaze unseeingly at the orchestra.

She sat with her hands folded calmly in her lap, her face serene, her posture impeccable, but her composure was only skin-deep. And Marc didn't make matters any easier. She made the mistake of putting an arm on the armrest and Marc took immediate advantage, covering her hand with his, then running his thumb over the back of her hand in erotic slow motion, tracing the curves and hollows and sending her pulse into orbit.

By the end of the concert, she was trembling with expectation. When Marc draped her coat around her shoulders, she was engulfed by his masculinity. She inhaled his musky fragrance and felt a delicious dizziness overcome her. She was surrounded by warmth, hemmed in by the heat of his large body. She raised mute eyes and stared at him, assaulted by alien longings.

"Did you enjoy it?" he murmured in a low voice.

For a moment she wondered what he meant—the music or his touch—then shook herself. "It was lovely."

His eyes held hers as a slow, knowing smile tilted one side of his mouth. "Yes," he murmured, one strong arm around her. "It was..."

He led her up the crowded aisle, nodding and smiling to acquaintances here and there, and she supposed she did the same. Somewhere off in space she heard her voice, heard her own laughter, saw people stopping to chat, but nothing was real except Marc's large body so near hers, sheltering her from reality, binding her in a kind of trance. She was profoundly aware of his arm around her, the sound of his low, melodious voice and his laughter.

And she was profoundly aware of herself, of her body and its unfamiliar new quirks. Something strange was going on inside her. She was filled with warmth, yet little shivers rippled through her. Perhaps that accounted for the burgeoning hardness of her nipples, which seemed to thrust hungrily through the lace of her bra as if searching for greater tactile pleasures. The slight whisper of her nylon-clad thighs as she walked seemed magnified a thousand times.

A heavy languor swept over her and she had to fight the impulse to turn toward Marc and melt against him. She seemed filled with the impulse to *kiss*, as if her body were suddenly rebelling from its lean diet and crying out for rich food. One question preoccupied her, so that she nodded and smiled and laughed, but inside she kept wondering when she had last kissed a man. Nothing seemed more important than that, except perhaps her wish for Marc to kiss her.

She was shocked by her thoughts and tried desperately to control them, but then they were outside and Marc's arm was around her even more tightly, pulling her closer against him. "My God," he said roughly, "I've never seen so many people I know in one place in my life. I've never wanted to get out of a place so badly. I wanted to..."

He broke off and his eyes seemed to devour her. She felt herself sinking into them, felt her body melting against his, nerveless and boneless. Her eyelids grew heavy and the warmth inside her heated up, swirling until her stomach was a pinwheel of expectation.

"What did you want, Marc?" she whispered.

His eyes drew her in, sweeping her into a whirlwind of desire. His lips came down ever so slowly, and her head tilted back ever so slightly, and for a moment, time halted, as if suspended in midair. He started to kiss her when Smitty materialized out of nowhere, whacking Marc heartily on the back and grabbing Monica's hand and pumping it up and down energetically.

"So! Did you guys enjoy the concert?" Smitty boomed, looking from one to the other expectantly.

A combination of ground glass and gunpowder merged in Marc's voice. "No. It was lousy. What the hell are you doing here?"

Smitty spread his hands, looking like an abashed puppy. "Hey, can I help it if I wanna get culture? I see my friends, I wanna say hello." He looked from Marc to Monica.

He was turning away when Monica reached out and caught his arm. "Smitty...."

He turned back, looking aggrieved. "Yeah?"

His interruption had totally destroyed the mood and the moment. It might never happen again, she realized, but that was no excuse for treating Smitty rudely. She reached out and smoothed a hand over his crumpled lapel. "Nothing," she murmured. "Just hello."

Marc's expression softened. He grasped Smitty's hand in a firm handshake. "The concert was great, Smitty. I'm sorry I snapped at you."

Monica glanced at him warmly from behind Smitty's balding head. Somehow, seeing Marc's chagrin and his effort to make amends to Smitty was even nicer than if he'd kissed her. She smiled, snuggling her chin into the luxurious fur collar of her coat.

Wouldn't it be strange, she thought, if she actually started to like the guy...?

"That was kind of you," Marc said when they were ensconced in his sports car ten minutes later. "Smitty was the last person I wanted to see right then. I'm afraid I had other things on my mind like how nice it would be to kiss you. I'm afraid those good genes of mine you're so crazy about didn't do me any good—my manners went straight to hell." He paused for a red light and looked at Monica thoughtfully. "But maybe good manners aren't a product of genes."

Monica snuggled into the corner of her seat, her head tilted slightly as she studied Marc. Her equilibrium was back and she felt in control of herself once more. She chuckled lazily. "Is this part of your game plan, Marc? Are you trying to convince me that I heat up your blood so much you lose all ability to cope socially?"

For a moment he seemed almost hurt, then one corner of his mouth lifted in wry humor. "Uh-huh," he drawled lazily, taking off and shifting smoothly through the gears. "You make me lose all control, Monica. Always did. You're so damned cool, so composed, and I'm just a mass of quivering nerves."

"Just like a school kid," she teased softly.

"You got it." He glanced at her, his teeth flashing whitely in a grin. "You won't make it easy for me, will you, Monica?"

"Wouldn't be much fun for you otherwise, would it? I mean, it's the challenge you men like, isn't it? The pursuit of the prey?"

"Is that what you think this is? A matter of scoring with you? Male pride and all that?"

She shrugged lightly. "Isn't it?"

He was quiet as he maneuvered the small sports car onto the highway, merging with the fast-moving traffic. "If I remember correctly, Monica, you called me. You initiated all this. You can't blame a man for trying to take advantage of a situation that's been neatly deposited in his lap, can you?"

Monica felt her heart take an incredible dip, then she lifted her chin. What had she expected? That he'd admit to some long-standing crush on her? "Well," she said, unable to keep from smarting at his words, "I'm glad you're not trying to lay a line on me. I think honesty is definitely the best policy between us."

"Everything nice and clean and tidy, is that it, Monica?"

"Precisely," she said, turning in her seat to face forward. Suddenly she no longer felt in control. She was unaccountably annoyed but wasn't sure who or what she was annoyed at.

"No emotions, no entanglements, no feelings, right?" Marc prodded.

She sneaked a glance at him, and saw that he looked carefree and unconcerned, and for some reason, that made her almost angry. "What's the problem, Marc?" she taunted. "Does it bother you that I'm not being swept off my feet? Is it a blow to that colossal male ego of yours to find out that you can't seduce me in six easy steps?"

"Six easy steps?" he asked mildly, glancing at her with amused eyes. "I may not count too well, but to my way of thinking, I haven't even made one move yet, much less six."

"You mean that seduction scene at the Bushnell tonight wasn't calculated to melt my bones?"

"Seduction scene?" he asked innocently.

"Oh, come off it, Marc," she snorted. "All that holding my hand and leaning over and whispering in my ear and that delicious cologne you must have bathed in." She gave him a knowing look. "Did you really think I'd fall for all that corny stuff?"

He raised his shoulders in a bewildered shrug. "I'm not exactly sure what you mean, Monica. I don't think I treated you any differently tonight than any other woman I take out."

That momentarily shook her. She adjusted her face to hide her confusion and gave him a radiant smile. "Good," she purred. "I wouldn't want to think you were using your big guns to so little effect."

"Honey," Marc drawled, pulling his car to a stop in front of her condominium, "So far I haven't even loaded a derringer, much less called out the big guns." He cut the engine and turned to face her, reaching out to brush a stray curl from her cheek. "But when I do," he said, his voice suddenly lower and entirely too enticing, "I'll be sure to let you know so you can erect your defenses."

She shivered under his light touch and told herself to get out of the car, but for some reason her body wouldn't move. She felt a slow-moving fire begin to burn in her midsection, radiating outward in delicious waves, heating her blood so it seemed to pulse though her veins in warming confusion. Her breathing grew shallow and she was suddenly exquisitely aware of how quickly her breasts were rising and falling. Did Marc notice, too?

An aching quiet descended on the car, broken only by the suddenly magnified sound of her breathing. Marc brushed his fingers lightly back and forth across her cheek, then eased them into the thickness of her hair which lay unbound on her shoulders in plentiful silver-blond waves.

"You have beautiful hair," he murmured as if talking to himself. Slowly he lifted a strand and let it sift through his fingers. She shivered again as the silk of her hair fell onto her bare skin, and Marc began a slow, intimate massage of the tight cords in the back of her neck.

His fingers brushed the nape of her neck, sending electrical charges that seemed to short-circuit through her senses. "Beautiful skin," he murmured, his voice low and hypnotic. "It feels like silk under my fingertips." He leaned forward and brushed his nose against the ripe curve where her shoulder joined her neck. "Lilacs," he whispered. "You remind me of lilacs in May."

She closed her eyes and felt her head fall back as his lips brushed the soft skin just under her ear. His breath was warm as his lips hovered over her skin, tantalizing with only the promise of kisses. Her lips parted, allowing a soft sigh to escape. She moved her hand up the rough texture of Marc's suit coat, feeling the hard contour of his muscled chest beneath the smoothness of his shirt.

She couldn't speak, couldn't move. Mutely, she tried to shake off her mood. "I think I'd better go in, Marc."

He brushed his fingertips lightly down her cheek and ran his eyes over her face. "You don't want me to kiss you?"

She managed to find her voice. "I want to go in," she whispered, and was mortified to hear how shaky her voice was, how feather-soft, how filled with yearning and desire. Her words had said one thing, but her voice had betrayed her, just as her body was betraying her. Marc knew what she really wanted, just as she did. All he had to do was lean forward just a couple of inches more.

He hovered near her lips for a second, then lifted his head. Searching her eyes, Marc studied her, then sat back. "All right," he said, his own voice oddly husky. "I'll take you in. No good-night kisses, no caresses."

She felt everything fall inside her. Mutely she stared at him, her eyes large and filled with silent disappointment. He stared back, waiting, watching, then opened his door and got out of the car.

She sat in the car, struggling to control her disappointment and hunger, and find some shred of dignity to hold on to. When he opened the door, she got out of the car and bent her head, as if preoccupied with searching in her pocketbook for her keys.

Marc took her arm and escorted her to the door. "Lovely night," he said, sounding cheerful and unconcerned.

At the door, Monica turned and studied him. She was in control again, but her body still tingled with sexual tension. She took a quiet, calming breath and put out her hand. "Marc," she said, nodding formally.

He stared at her hand, then took it in a firm handshake. "Monica." He stretched a mock bow over her hand. "I'll pick you up at six forty-five tomorrow. Curtain's at seven-thirty."

She withdrew her hand and turned and unlocked the door.

"Good night, Monica."

She didn't even bother to turn around. "Good night, Marc," she said coolly, then closed the door quietly. Once inside, she let out her pent-up breath and sank back against the door. Her legs were wobbly and her stomach a mass of tangled butterflies. She took a shaky breath and closed her eyes.

"Oh, God," she whispered, opening her eyes to stare unseeingly ahead. "What have I got myself into?"

Four

Laughter punctuated the low murmur of conversation in the lobby of the Hartford Stage Company as Monica smiled and nodded to acquaintances. She was supremely aware of Marc's strong hand on her back, guiding her toward the theater entrance where two teenagers passed out programs and took tickets. He was wearing that provocative cologne again, and was dressed tonight in a blue Harris tweed jacket and gray slacks, looking properly upscale, like the rest of the well-dressed crowd.

"I like your dress," Marc said, bending to whisper in her ear.

Monica felt her pulse accelerate momentarily. "Thank you," she murmured, feeling a soft glow permeate her body. It felt good wearing this pink wool dress with her pearls. It was very different from her usual cashmere or wool business suits, and made her feel distinctly feminine. Or was that

Marc's doing? She tried not to think about that question, but actually nothing else had been on her mind all day.

They settled into their seats, and Monica tried to collect herself as Marc talked with a friend. She stared at the curtainless stage that protruded into the theater, outwardly inspecting the set but really listening to the tenor of Marc's voice. She found herself smiling at the way he laughed. It was a husky laugh, filled with honest amusement and good humor, the kind of laugh that was catching.

"Will it be any good?" Marc's low voice interrupted her reverie.

Startled, she looked into his eyes and felt a pleasurable lurch in her midsection. "Will what be any good?" she asked.

Humor lit up his eyes as they searched hers. "The play."

"The reviews were good."

"Oh, well, theater reviews," he said dismissingly. "Everyone knows they're written by members of the Chamber of Commerce. Regional theaters are struggling, and the newspapers and business community are in cahoots with them. It's kind of a conspiracy to try to bring culture to the masses. You wouldn't get an honest opinion of a regional theater production in a local newspaper if your life depended on it. They're like book reviews."

She arched an amused brow. "Book reviews?"

"Book reviews," he repeated. "Ever really read them? Every writer is uncommonly something or other. Uncommonly knowledgeable about life, or uncommonly wise, or uncommonly gifted." He shook his head. "I hate that word—uncommonly."

She rested her elbow on the armrest between them and propped her chin on her hand, her eyes sparkling. "What else do you want to get off your chest? Do you have any grudges against ballet? The symphony?" She shrugged lightly. "The latest blockbuster movie?"

He took her hand and tucked it into the crook of his arm. "All right," he said, laughing comfortably, "I'll get off my soapbox."

"No," she protested, her eyes searching his. "Don't. I like to listen to you." Her teasing laughter faded, and she suddenly felt awkward. She remembered feeling like this on dates in college, wondering what to say and how to say it. It was incredible that a sophisticated thirty-five-year-old woman could still suffer from the same insecurities she had fifteen years ago. "I didn't mean to make fun of what you were saying, Marc," she said softly. "I really was enjoying listening to you."

"Were you?" His low voice sent a pleasant shiver over her skin as he moved his thumb caressingly across the back of her hand. The house lights flickered, signaling that the play would begin soon. Marc glanced around, then smiled imtimately into her eyes. "I'll have to continue during intermission then."

She didn't answer, just sat staring into his eyes, feeling that magical sense of excitement and expectation flower within her. When the lights dipped and the play began, she found she couldn't concentrate. Marc was too near, his hand too warm on hers, the movement of his thumb too erotic as he stroked the inside of her wrist. She took a silent deep breath, trying to get her equilibrium back, but instead she inhaled Marc's scent, which set her pulses pounding and made her mouth go dry.

Marc leaned toward her. "You okay?"

She felt her heart lurch. Was her distraction that noticeable? "I'm fine," she murmured.

He moved his thumb over her wrist again. "You sure?"

His low voice acted on her senses like velvet on naked skin. She felt a strange pulsing begin within her, felt a wave of heat move up from her breasts into the creamy skin of her neck. She took a steadying breath. "Mmm-hmm."

Marc didn't say anything, but she sensed rather than saw that his lips curved into a complacent smile. Immediately she felt her backbone stiffen. She was damned if she'd sit here and miss the play because she was mooning like a love-struck teenager. Calmly, she pulled her hand from Marc's and placed her elbows firmly on the armrests, steepling her fingers in her most professional manner and fixing her eyes coolly on the actors.

"What was the last line?" Marc asked in an undertone.

She hesitated. "I don't know," she admitted finally. "I missed it too."

"Were you thinking of something else?" he asked, a bit too innocently.

His voice challenged her to look at him. She sat staring at the actors until she finally couldn't stand it any longer. She turned her head and met his gaze. "Yes," she said, thankful for her outward calm. "I was."

Someone shifted in the seat behind them and they fell silent, but it took another five minutes before Monica was able to concentrate on the play. It took exactly five seconds for her to be completely fixated on Marc when the first act ended and the house lights went up.

"Would you like a glass of wine?"

She nodded and walked with him up the steps toward the mezzanine level. He guided her toward the bar, where a small crowd had already gathered. Photographs of the stage production lined the walls, and muted conversation and laughter filled the air. While Marc got their drinks, Monica strolled along the walls, studying the photographs with outward interest, but not seeing them at all.

She was thinking about Marc, thinking about her reaction to him, remembering what this was all about. Frowning thoughtfully, she came to a stop and stared at a photograph of two of the actors. It was odd how it had become a kind of challenge to her not to give in to him, almost as if it were a point of honor. But now she realized she was fighting herself as well as Marc. Why? What would be so horrible about having a pleasant little interlude between the sheets with Marc? He'd get to sleep with her, she'd get her baby, and they would both be happy. . . .

"You look puzzled," Marc said from very close to her. "Can I help you understand the play perhaps? Offer you a little intelligent interpretation of character motivation? Give you my theory of what the playwright's trying to say?"

Smiling, she turned to him and took the glass he held out. "Why not," she said lightly, taking a sip of the white wine. "What's the playwright trying to say?"

He frowned with mock pretentiousness. "Cosmic nothingness," he said, gesturing to the actors in the photograph in front of them. "They symbolize man's inability to communicate. The lack of plot symbolizes lack of meaning in modern life. Damned sophisticated stuff. Better than Rogers and Hart, don't you think?"

She found herself laughing softly. "Now why do I get the feeling that you'd prefer Rogers and Hart?"

"You mean it shows?" He searched her eyes. "Do you like it? The play?"

"Not really," she admitted, then looked around at the bright and beautiful people, all posturing and laughing elegantly. It was a brittle sound, she thought, and incredibly false. "I'll bet not many of them do either, but we're all afraid to say so for sounding unsophisticated." She cocked her head and studied Marc. "But you surprise me. You look so. . . ." She trailed off, trying to figure out what she really thought of Marc.

"So what, Monica? Worldly? Sophisticated? Intelligent?"

"Mmm," she murmured in an ironic undertone, noncommittal and teasing at the same time. She turned back to the photograph. "I would have thought you'd like modern theater."

"Don't get me wrong, some of it is fascinating. It's just . . ." His eyes wandered her face admiringly. "It's hard to get into this play. I'm afraid you'll have to take the blame for that."

"Me?" Suddenly she felt almost nervous. Why did he constantly do this to her? By shifting things to a personal level he threw her into confusion.

"Mmm," he murmured, sounding almost drowsy. "I can't seem to get your perfume out of my mind." He reached out and brushed a strand of silvery blond hair back from her face. "What is it?"

"My perfume?" she asked, sounding oddly breathless. She couldn't look away from his eyes, couldn't escape the heat in them, couldn't ignore the feel of his fingers against her cheek.

"Yes, your perfume. What is it?"

"Obsession."

"Mmm," he finally said. "That's a terrific name for a perfume." He sipped his drink, his eyes still holding hers over the rim of the glass. Electricity seemed to sparkle in the air between them. He held her eyes with his, then dropped his gaze to her lips.

She felt her stomach turn in a somersault, felt heat invade her body in a shimmering wave of erotic delight. She seemed oddly heavy, as if weighted down with sensuality. She remembered feeling this way one hot, humid day in the Caribbean off Puerto Rico. The water had washed over her in warm, sensual waves, and she had sunk into it, her eyes closed, her lips softly parted, her entire body on fire with physical awareness. She'd floated in a dreamlike state, at one with the water and soft tropical air, mesmerized by physical longings she'd never before felt with a man.

Until now.

"More wine?" Marc's low voice floated into her consciousness.

She almost started, then lifted her gaze. "No, thank you, I'm fine."

"You were somewhere far away," he said softly.

She continued staring into his eyes, carefully assessing the effect he had on her. "Yes," she said finally. "I was swimming in Puerto Rico."

"I wish I'd been there with you," he said.

She took an unsteady breath. "Mmm," she murmured noncommittally, sipping her wine. "That would have been interesting."

The play dragged on interminably but finally ended. The applause was restrained and polite, then they were outside on the street, diagonally across from the civic center. Marc tucked her hand in the crook of his elbow, and they strolled along the sidewalk, heading for one of the restaurants in another of Hartford's new high-rise buildings.

"It's all so different now," Monica said, looking around at the buildings which towered around them. "I remember when I was a girl coming into Hartford one night to see a movie with a friend." She laughed softly. "That was when they still *had* movie theaters in Hartford."

"Careful, Monica," Marc teased. "Your age is showing."

She smiled, but went on with her musings. "It was so quiet that night, and the streets were deserted. We'd seen Hitchcock's *Psycho*, and when we got out of the theater her father hadn't arrived to pick us up, so we walked around the block. It was scary, especially after seeing that movie, but at the same time, you couldn't possibly believe that anything bad could happen in Hartford. It was such a small, friendly little city. But now..." She took a wistful breath and looked around. "Now it's all changed. The developers have gotten a hold of it and they won't be content until there isn't a scrap of undeveloped property. I know—I work with one of the biggest—Clay Firestone."

"You're sounding frighteningly conservative," Marc teased. "And here I thought you were on the side of the enlightened. What are you doing practicing real-estate law and representing Clayton Firestone with an attitude like that?"

"Sometimes I think I'd like to get out of law altogether. I take on divorce cases and wonder why in heaven's name anyone would ever take a chance and get married, and the more I see of real-estate developers, the more I dislike what they do as well. Hartford was a nice city the way it was, Marc. The only reason they're developing it is to make money. Oh, sure, they say it's progress and all that, but it isn't. It's profit, pure and simple."

"Do you really mean that about marriage?" Marc asked.

"What?" What was he talking about? She'd been talking about real-estate developers.

"Did you really mean what you said about wondering why people ever get married?"

"Did I say that?" She was completely startled.

"You most certainly did. You said the more divorce cases you take on, the more you wonder how anyone could be foolish enough to get married."

"Oh. That must have just slipped out." She laughed ironically. "I didn't need to practice law to feel that way. I felt that way growing up."

"Oh?"

Marc had paused for her to continue, but she changed the subject. She wasn't about to "open up." She'd always thought that revealing personal matters displayed weakness. Some things you just didn't talk about—and unhappy marriages like her parents' was one of those things.

"I'm famished," she said. "It's amazing how sitting in a theater can whip up an appetite. This week spent wining and dining me is going to send you into bankruptcy."

"You let me worry about that," Marc said, holding open the door to the restaurant. "You just sit back and enjoy yourself."

"I've always thought women get off too easily in the dating game," she said when they had settled at a table.

"Oh?" Marc glanced up from the menu, looking almost startled.

"Yes. Why should we be the ones to get all the money spent on us? It doesn't seem fair."

"I suppose that's why some women think men want something more than a good-night kiss at the end of the night," Marc commented dryly.

"Don't you?" she challenged.

"Is that directed at men in general or me in particular?" he asked, his eyes gleaming with amusement.

She rested her elbow on the table and her chin in her hand and met his gaze directly. "Both."

"I can't speak for men in general," Marc said, "but I've never expected anything at the end of a date."

"Baloney," Monica said lazily.

"What do you mean?"

"You expected something at the end of our date two years ago."

"That's because I thought you'd be interested."

She was taken aback by his answer. She slowly straightened. "Oh? Why would you think that?"

"You seemed properly repressed, and I guess I thought you might like to indulge in a few sinful pleasures with a strong, healthy, red-blooded guy like me."

"Repressed!"

He shrugged. "Granted, it's stereotypical thinking, but you look like an ice maiden, Monica, and you act like one. You used to pile that silvery hair in a sedate little bun, and you wear those businesslike suits—yet you've got great legs, a wonderful body, and a face that could stop traffic on 42nd Street. A guy gets to fantasizing about a woman like you.''

"Fantasizing," she said wonderingly.

"Exactly. At least I did. I began to wonder what it would be like to take those pins out of your hair and see it spill over your bare shoulders." He tilted his head, his gaze speculative. She shivered at the look in his eyes, and realized too late she'd opened a hornet's nest.

Marc sat forward, his eyes filled with smoky sexuality. "I used to picture taking you to bed with me, Monica," he said huskily. "In my daydreams, you did the most outlandish things."

She swallowed with great difficulty, then ducked her head and studied the menu with unseeing eyes. "Did I," she mused, and realized too late that her own voice sounded unusually low, almost sexy. She took a calming breath and told herself he was teasing her. She couldn't let him get to her. "It would be a shame to spoil those daydreams, Marc," she said absently, pretending to concentrate on the menu. She lifted her eyes and smiled sweetly. "Reality is always so disappointing, don't you think?"

"I don't think it would be disappointing with you, Monica."

She wished she had her glasses with her. She would set them on the end of her nose and peer over the frames. That would surely destroy this utterly dangerous mood. Lacking horn-rimmed spectacles, she'd just pretend he hadn't said anything. "I think I'll have the appetizer platter of oysters on the half shell and shrimp cocktail," she said, looking up and smiling. "And another drink."

"Oysters are considered aphrodisiacs," Marc said idly. "Did you know that?"

Her eyes swerved from his. "Really." She fixed a smile on her face and pretended to look at a potted plant.

"Part of my fantasies involved you and me eating oysters."

Startled, she looked back at him. "Really?"

"Mmm." One corner of his mouth lifted lazily. "While we were in bed together."

"Oysters," she repeated blankly. "In *bed*?"

"And in the hot tub. But those were just fantasies," he said offhandedly. "You don't want to hear about them, I'm sure."

She shook her head, feeling dazed. "No... no, of course not." She forced a smile and tried to get her balance back. "Hot tub?" The question came out so suddenly, she didn't even know she'd said it until it was out. Stunned at herself, she felt heat begin to rise into her face.

"A friend of mine has a beach house in Carmel, right on the Pacific. It's very Californian—hot tubs and romantic sunsets. I used to picture us there."

"I see." She moved her spoon a quarter of an inch to the right and repositioned her knife. "And um... do you have a hot tub? At your place?"

"Me?" Marc looked completely innocent. "No," he said, shaking his head. "No hot tubs."

Quiet descended, which was not a good thing. Into the silence came the image of a hot tub at a beach house in Carmel overlooking the Pacific. It was easy to picture herself in it with Marc. Monica shifted uneasily in her chair. Marc stared fixedly at his wine glass.

"Do you?" Marc asked suddenly.

"Do I what?"

"Have a hot tub?"

"Me?" She laughed nervously. "Uh-uh. I'm as straight as they come, Marc. I'm afraid your fantasies were just that. The closest I'll ever get to a hot tub is a decorating magazine."

"A shower would do."

She stared at him, nonplussed, then rearranged the salt and pepper shakers, pushed the sugar bowl to the left, and smoothed out a wrinkle in the linen tablecloth. She had to get him off the subject of his fantasies, fascinating as they might be. "What do you do for fun, Marc? Besides day-dreaming."

He ignored her jab and said, "Tennis, golf, sailing. What about you?"

"I play a little golf and tennis," she said, "but antiques are my real love."

"That surprises me. You live in a modern condominium. If you love antiques so much, why don't you have an old colonial house?"

"What would I need with a big old house?" she asked. "Anyway, I like the look of antiques in modern homes. The contrast is wonderful. Antiques warm up the white walls, which in turn show off the wood tones of the antiques."

"What about when you have a baby?"

His question startled her into complete silence. She stared at him, and for the first time what she was contemplating doing became real. Before, it had been just an idea; sud-denly it was reality. "I hadn't thought about that," she said slowly.

"I wonder if there's a lot you haven't thought about, Monica."

She stared at him, then sat back when the waiter depos-ited an ironstone platter filled with oysters and shrimp on the table. She stared at the seafood layered on crushed ice, surrounded by lemon wedges, parsley sprigs, and small pewter jars of seafood cocktail sauce. The waiter placed two small forks on the table and departed.

"I'm sorry, Monica," Marc said. "I shouldn't have said that. I'm sure you've thought everything out, and figured out the consequences right down to the cost of disposable diapers."

She frowned. "But that's just it, Marc," she said slowly. "I haven't. I haven't given one thought to where I—I mean, where we would live, the baby and I. And school. I'd have to pick a town with a good school system, and..." She raised her eyes slowly to Marc. "My whole life would change."

He nodded, his eyes serious.

She looked away, then reached for an oyster and washed it down with a sip of her drink. "But it would be a good change," she said, as if trying to convince herself. "I've thought a lot about the baby itself. I'd like a little girl, but a boy would be fine too, but—"

"You aren't worried about a boy needing a father around?"

She shook her head irritatedly at his interruption. "Of course not. There are plenty of single mothers who are raising boys just fine without fathers. No, it's just the idea of having a *baby*, Marc, and watching it grow up." She ran her finger around the rim of her glass, her face softening in a tender smile. "Taking her to nursery school in the morning, and being a den mother for brownies and Girl Scouts, and if she wanted ballet lessons, or art lessons, or wanted to play softball or soccer...whatever she wanted to do, that would be fine with me."

Her smile faded, and suddenly she was talking about herself, and she didn't know how it happened. "It wasn't like that for me, Marc. They never had time for me. Dad was too busy with work, and my mother was..."

"Was what?" Marc prompted gently.

Monica fiddled with her drink. What could she say about her mother? "She was, um, unhappy. She told me once that when she married my father she was crazy about him, but she realized she'd made a mistake by the time I was born. She never saw him. He lived and breathed his law practice." She raised serious eyes and studied Marc, then she found herself telling him something she'd never told anyone. "She drank, Marc. I'd come home from school and find her sitting in the den with a glass in her hand, just sitting there in the dark, staring out the windows."

Monica looked into the past, seeing the palatial white house that sat far back from a country road on fifteen acres in Farmington. The rooms were quiet and smelled of furniture wax and fresh flowers. There was a curving banister on the gracious staircase in the wide central foyer, and as a child she'd ridden down it for hours, whooping with delight, until her father had discovered her one night when he arrived home with an important client, and sent her sternly to her room. All joy, all laughter had been banished from that house. There she'd learned to permanently associate pleasure with guilt.

"The backyard was immense," Monica said slowly. "Mother would sit in the den and look out the windows at the flower beds and lawns which were tended by the gardening service. I remember one day I went in the den after school, and she turned her head when she saw me and smiled very distantly..." Monica felt hypnotized by the past, drawn into the memory by something she couldn't quite name.

"She was a beautiful woman," she continued slowly, "with magnificent ash blond hair she wore in a chignon and flawless skin and this utterly patrician manner." Monica frowned. "But this day she said to me, 'Monica, after I had you, I ceased to be of any use around here.' She lifted her glass and gestured out the windows. 'Look out there,' she said. 'It's beautiful, and I hate every bit of it.'"

Monica's brow wrinkled. She hadn't thought of that in years. Why was she talking about it now? "I didn't know it then, of course, but she was an alcoholic. I used to think alcoholics were the bums you'd see on the streets in the south end of Hartford, with bottles in brown paper bags and dirty clothes and filthy hair. *They* were alcoholics, not my mother."

"It must have been rough on you," Marc said gently.

The gentleness in his voice acted like a dose of cold water. Monica wasn't used to gentleness, didn't trust it. Immediately she snapped out of the past. She'd said too much already, anyway. "I managed," she said lightly, and picked up a shrimp and dipped it in cocktail sauce. "What was your childhood like?"

"Happy," Marc, said, smiling. "Apparently the direct opposite of yours."

"Were you a paperboy?" Monica asked quickly. Now that she'd said too much, she was ashamed, and wanted only to divert Marc's thoughts from her own life.

"Matter of fact, I was," Marc said. "And a Boy Scout, too."

"I bet you even helped little old ladies cross busy streets," Monica teased.

"I believe I did," Marc said with strange seriousness. "And ever since, I've had a soft spot for women in trouble."

Monica slowly lifted her eyes and met his gaze. The smile on her face faded. "Don't, Marc. Don't make the mistake of thinking I need you. I don't need anyone. I never have and I never will."

"But you do need me, Monica," Marc said softly, amusement suddenly flickering in his eyes. "Or have you forgotten your—how shall I say it? Your predicament?"

Five

When they walked back to the parking garage, it was well after midnight, and the streets were deserted. Monica shivered at the chill night air and pulled her collar up around her neck.

"Cold?" Marc asked.

"A little."

He put his arm around her and began to rub her back in warming circles. "Better?"

She pulled away, her face closed up. "My coat's warm enough, thank you."

Sighing, Marc dropped his arm and shoved his hands into his trouser pockets and began to whistle. Monica kept her gaze straight ahead, her head high. She'd let her guard down a bit tonight and had to compensate. It wouldn't do to let him think she was some silly, vulnerable woman who couldn't take care of herself. She'd taken care of herself all her life, and for the past twelve years, she'd lived on her own. Marc might be right about her needing him for reproductive purposes, but that was all she needed him for.

For some reason, Marc had fallen behind her. She turned and saw incredulously that he was doing a soft-shoe routine in the middle of the sidewalk, whistling jauntily and tapping up a storm, his hands still in his pockets, his elbows akimbo. All he needed was a snap-brim hat cocked rakishly over his eye. She stood there staring, not quite knowing how to react, then the absurdity of the situation hit her.

She crossed her arms and leaned against a store front, amusement flickering in her eyes. Marc finally realized she was watching and stopped dancing, favoring her with a huge grin.

"Like it?" he asked.

"Not particularly," she said dryly.

"No? What part didn't you like? The whistling? The dance steps?"

"You need a hat, first of all," she said, trying to keep from laughing. "And a cane."

"And rain," Marc added, grinning. "Gene Kelly looked better because he was dancing in the rain."

"Mmm, you have a point," Monica conceded, "but then he wasn't whistling in the rain, he was singing."

"Mmm," Marc said, frowning thoughtfully. By this time, he'd reached her side. He threw back his head and began to sing in a lusty off-key baritone. He began to do a shuffling soft-shoe again, then whirled around a lamp post. "Well?" he asked, beaming at her, one arm thrown out in a flourish. "What d'ya think?"

Monica looked behind him at the police cruiser that had pulled up. A policeman sat staring at Marc, incredulity stamped on his beefy face. "I don't know," she said. "What do *you* think, officer?"

Marc whirled around. "Oh, God," he said, and threw Monica a sheepish look. "Now he'll book me for disturbing the peace or something and I'll make the papers and lose my job."

"That you, Mr. English?" the policeman asked.

Marc turned and bent over and peered into the cruiser. "Hey, Tiny! How're you doin'?" He straightened and gestured for Monica to join him. "This is Tiny," he said, indicating the huge black man who probably weighed close to three hundred pounds. "Tiny, this is Ms. Bliss. She'd probably want you to run me in just so she can get rid of me."

Tiny laughed. "He botherin' you, Miss? We can put him away a *long* time if he is. We got all kinds of tricks up our sleeves to rid the world of misfits."

Monica looked from Tiny to Marc, then shook her head, her eyes gleaming with mischief. "That's okay, Tiny, I think I can cope until he brings me home."

"That would be just as well," Tiny said, grinning. "We don't wanna lose the one lawyer round these parts who does his job."

"Careful, Tiny," Marc said. "Ms. Bliss is an attorney, too."

"Uh-oh," Tiny said, adjusting his face to look serious. "Just a joke, Ms. Bliss. Just a little joke."

"I understand, Tiny," Monica said, laughing softly. "No offense."

He tipped his hat to her and grinned at Marc, and glided away from the sidewalk, the radio in his cruiser crackling with static and muffled conversation.

Marc put a hand on Monica's elbow and guided her across the street toward the parking garage. "Did I embarrass you?"

"No, as a matter of fact, you didn't."

"You sound surprised."

"I am," she admitted.

"I'm glad, Monica," Marc said quietly, his eyes filled with warmth.

They came to a stop near the darkened entrance to the garage and just stared into each others' eyes. "I'm sorry, Marc," she finally said.

"Sorry?" he asked, looking confused. "For what?"

"For being such a jerk. You put your arm around me to be a gentleman and try to warm me up, and I almost took your arm off at the elbow."

He put his hands up, palms toward her. "Hey, no apologies necessary. Let's forget it, okay?"

She nodded, and slowly smiled. "Okay," she murmured.

He stood there looking at her, then slowly lowered his head and kissed her. It took her completely by surprise. She hadn't expected it, and it was over so quickly she began to wonder if she'd imagined the whole thing.

"That's not the way I'd planned to kiss you the first time," Marc said softly.

"No?"

He shook his head, his eyes filled with heat. "Our first kiss was gonna be world-class. I would have hired violins if I could, and moonlight and roses and champagne..." He reached out and touched her hair, letting it sift through his fingers. "But all of a sudden, strategy doesn't seem to matter. I just want to kiss you, and hold you."

She couldn't look away from his eyes. "Then why don't you?" she whispered.

Groaning softly, he took her in his arms. She went willingly, pliantly, her body all warmth and responsiveness. She wrapped her arms around his neck and went up on tiptoe, straining toward him, to that elemental male warmth that acted like a flame to her femininity. His lips were sweet and demanding, no longer gentle yet not hurtful. They moved over hers in erotic supplication, probing, caressing, seeking, until her own lips parted, allowing his tongue entrance.

She almost gasped with pleasure when he slid his tongue over and around hers in voluptuous exploration. Finally they parted, but he continued to hold her pressed against him, his arms strong around her, his breath sweet on her ear. Her heart pounded erratically against his chest and she closed her eyes and clung to him, her cheek pressed into the rough tweed of his jacket, her senses assailed by his masculinity, his cologne, the feel of his strong body.

Finally he released her and she stood back, confusedly pushing a strand of hair from her face. "No violins," she said with a soft, nervous laugh. "But it wasn't bad as first kisses go."

He seemed about to take her in his arms again, but he took a deep breath, as if reasserting control and said, "Time to get you home." Taking her hand, he led her into the parking garage. "Don't cook supper tomorrow night, okay?"

"Why?" she asked, smiling. "You taking me someplace special?"

"No," he answered. "I'm cooking you dinner."

"You!"

"Monica, don't look so startled. I can cook. In fact, I'm a darned good cook. I'll have everything we'll need, even down to the right wine and candles."

"And where are we going to enjoy this epicurean repast? Your place or mine?"

"Yours." He unlocked the car door and looked up at her, his gray eyes sparkling. "Two years ago I noticed that you have a fireplace." He grinned at her. "That's a lot more romantic."

"I'll have a fire going then," she said, pausing to smile at him as she got in the car. "But don't expect a big, successful seduction scene, Mr. English. The way to this woman's heart ain't through her stomach."

Marc began to start the car after seating her, then hesitated, turning t
word her. "What *is* the way to your heart?"

She turned in the seat so she was facing him and cuddled into the corner of the plush leather bucket seat. "There isn't one," she said, her blue eyes laughing. "I'm immune."

"Now that sounds like a challenge," he said, starting the car and backing out.

"No, just the truth." She peered at Marc as he maneuvered the small sports car down the twisting-labyrinthine ramps of the parking garage. As they drove under the indoor lights, he was illuminated briefly, then they were cast into shadows. Thoughtfully she turned in her seat and faced forward. The kiss had been nice. It had been more than nice; it had knocked her shoes off and sent her senses reeling.

She lay her head back on the leather seat and closed her eyes, remembering it, remembering the feel of his lips, the heat of his tongue and the eager, desiring way he'd thrust it into her mouth, coaxing her into a response she hadn't dreamed she could give so readily. Just thinking of it made her feel weak with longing.

She wanted to reach out and put a hand on Marc's arm, and tell him to pull the car off the highway and take her in his arms again, kiss her again, more than kiss her. She wanted him to undress her, carry her into bed, and make slow, languorous love to her. She wanted to feel his lips on her breasts, feel that wonderful hot, seeking tongue of his on her nipples, trailing down her midriff to her navel, searching out her pulsing core.

And she wanted to undress him, unbutton that starched shirt, undo that perfectly knotted silk tie, unzip those immaculately pressed trousers, and slide her hands over the hair-roughened texture of his skin, feel the rise and fall of muscles under her palms, inhale his musky odor...

"Monica?"

His low voice pulled her from her reverie. She opened her eyes guiltily and rolled her head on the back of the seat toward him. "Yes?" Her own voice was low and feathery, filled with all the heat her fantasies had conjured up. She kept her head on the seat, staring at him with wide, heated eyes, her lips parted with the memory of her fantasies, her heart hammeringly loudly, her breasts rising and falling in silent, almost painful agitation.

"We're home," he said.

She didn't respond. She just sat staring at him, still feeling the effects of her erotic fantasies, her cheeks flushed with hectic color, the pupils large and dark in her china blue eyes. "I want you to kiss me again," she said softly.

His eyes traveled her face, as if searching for the truth, then he leaned forward. His lips hovered over hers, his breath warm and sweet, filled with a moist hint of eroticism. She moved her hands up his chest and curled her fingers into his lapels as the ache within her became more insistent. The sweet need quickened her breathing, tightening her nipples until they seemed to cry out for the touch of Marc's hands and lips.

And then he kissed her, moving and enticing, probing for her response until she melted against him, her soul filled with sweet yearning, her mind empty of everything but him. She shuddered as his lips opened over hers, as his tongue probed and found hers, mating with it, taking her breath away with a shock as energizing as icy water.

Everything swirled within her in dizzying response, and her head fell back as he slid his tongue along hers, sending waves of pleasure through her body. She grew weak, then dizzy, then strangely hot, filled with an incredible sweet ache, a need so tortured she felt on fire. He tightened his arms around her and pressed her against his chest and she gloried in the feel of her breasts against him, delighted in the sweet ache that permeated them.

She said his name shakily, drinking in calming breaths, trembling with a desire so intense she didn't know what to do, how to handle it, where to turn for release. "Kiss me again."

His lips moved over hers in expert kisses, nipping, probing, seeking. He moved his hands over her back, urging her to greater response. And then he eased them slowly, unerringly down her back, coming to rest on her side, his fingers splayed, the tip of his thumb just brushing the ripe curve of her breast.

It was sweet, exquisite torture. She knew she had only to melt into his arms and continue their kisses and he would touch her breasts. From there, all would be chaos. There would be no turning back, not the way she felt right now. She was on fire with need, all her repressed desires aching to burst out in one fiery consummation.

She wanted it so badly she was shaking, but some quiet inner strength intervened, allowing her to sit back, adjust her skirt, shake back her hair, and muster a friendly smile. "Thank you for the play and dinner, Marc. It was lovely."

He sat staring at her, his right arm draped over the back of her seat, his eyes speculative. Finally he seemed to make a mental shrug and reached over and opened her door. "I'll walk you to the door," he said, and was out of the car and around to her side in time to help her from her seat.

Without speaking, they walked to her doorway, shrouded by tall shrubs, illuminated dimly by a recessed light. The night was growing colder. Glittering shards of frost spangled the grass, giving it an ethereal, otherwordly appearance. No lights shone from the other condominiums. No leaves rustled in the slight breeze, no cars drove by, no voices cut the silence. All was quiet, silent, still.

At her door, Monica fitted the key into the lock with trembling fingers, then pushed open the door. The dim light in her foyer beckoned. She could invite him in for coffee. It would be simple, even courteous. They could build a fire in the fireplace. He would kiss her again. He would touch her perhaps, begin to unzip her dress . . .

She turned blindly and hurried into the safety of her home. "Goodnight, Marc."

"I'll see you tomorrow night," he said, sounding grave and quiet.

She looked back at him, startled. She'd forgotten about tomorrow night. He'd be here again, alone with her all night. Well, not *all* night. . . . "Yes," she said. "What time?"

"Seven?"

She looked at him from the safety of her foyer, wanting even now to reach out and take his hand, to pull him into the house and close the door.

"Seven will be fine," she managed.

He nodded gravely, then turned and walked back toward his car, shoving his hands into his pockets. She stood and watched, expecting him to whistle jauntily, as if to show her she hadn't affected him as he had her. But he didn't whistle. At the car, he stopped and looked back at her. She stood in the half-opened doorway, returning his look, poised on the edge of calling him back, then she shut the door and turned off the outside light.

A moment later, she heard his car drive off. Letting out a pent-up breath, she crept through the darkened house to her room.

"You're looking happy today, Ms. Bliss."

Surprised, Monica looked up at her secretary. "Am I, Terry?"

The young woman nodded, grinning. "You've been humming in here all day. I've never heard you so happy. Did you land a big account or something?"

Monica sat back in her plush leather chair and studied her secretary. "Have I really gotten so bad that the only thing that makes me happy is work?"

Terry shrugged, looking suddenly embarrassed. "Well, I don't know... I mean, you never talk about your personal life, so I guess I just assumed..." The young woman's face grew red. "I'm sorry, Ms. Bliss, I won't meddle from now on." She turned to go, but Monica's voice stopped her.

"Terry, why don't you call me Monica?"

Terry turned around slowly, astonishment wreathing her face. "What?"

"I think you should call me Monica," Monica said, shrugging. "We've worked together three years now. It's totally ridiculous that you should continue to call me Ms. Bliss."

"Well..." Terry smiled in confusion. "Well, thank you."

"It is kind of unnerving, isn't it?" Monica asked dryly. "Next you'll be wondering if I've lost my marbles."

"Oh, no, Ms. Bliss!—I mean, Monica."

Monica considered her secretary. "Would you sit down a minute?"

"Sure." Terry perched on the edge of a wing chair. "Is something wrong?"

Monica shook her head. "No," she said, smiling. "I've just been doing a lot of thinking lately. How would you feel if the work slowed down a little in the office?"

Terry stared, then swallowed uncomfortably. "Um, do you mean like I'd be laid off or something?"

"No! Good heavens, not in the least. I'm just thinking of taking a whole new slant in my work—doing less divorce and real-estate development deals and maybe getting into something else."

"Like what?"

"Well, nothing is really firmed up yet, but I'd like to begin working with conservancy groups and historical associations, maybe use my knowledge of real-estate law to work for preservation of historic buildings, instead of using it to help developers put up ugly high rises."

"Why, I think that'd be great," Terry said earnestly, her large brown eyes shining. "But no matter what you do, I want to continue working for you. You're great, Ms. Bliss."

Taken back, Monica studied her secretary. "I'm not too distant? Too..." she shrugged hesitantly. "Too cold?"

"Oh, Ms. Bliss," Terry said, laughing and waving away her words. "You're professional, that's all. I have friends who work in those big law firms downtown and you're a peach compared to what I hear about them. I mean, you get your own coffee, and you never expect me to do personal errands, you pay terrific, and you've never yelled at me—"

"Yelled at you?" Monica looked shocked.

"I've always felt like a *person* around you, Ms. Bliss. Calling each other by first names isn't what makes a good boss-employee relationship, you know." Terry cocked her head, her eyes sparkling. "But if it isn't work, is it a man?"

Monica stared. "A man?"

"Yeah. Is it a man that's made you so happy? Is that why you've been humming all day?"

"Good heavens, no!" Monica began transferring stacks of paper to other stacks, in a pretense of straightening her immaculate desk.

"I *knew* it was a man!" Terry squeaked. "Oh, I'm so happy for you, Ms. Bliss—Monica." The secretary's eyes glowed and she dropped her voice to a reverent whisper. "Are you getting married?"

"Married!" Monica stared. "Of course not! And how did you—I mean—"

Terry laughed away Monica's question. "Oh, come on, you're just like any other woman—absolutely transparent when it comes to matters of the heart."

"Matters of the—" Monica broke off. Was it really that obvious? She stared as Terry ran out the door to answer the phone, then swiveled her chair around and gazed out at the vivid splash of scarlet-and-gold maple leaves against the majestic mid-October sky.

She was doing it—she was getting involved. She'd known how dangerous that could be, especially with a man like Marc English. Now she'd have to redouble her efforts to hold him at bay. It was only four more days. Surely she could keep him at a safe distance for four little days....

When she opened the door to Marc five hours later, he greeted her with armloads of packages, thrusting a bouquet of vivid orange-red sweetheart roses into her hands, and kissing her hungrily on the lips from over the tops of mounds of grocery bags.

"Where's the kitchen?" he asked huskily, his lips moving against hers, his tongue flicking over her lips teasingly.

Shivering, she stepped back. "That way."

He deposited a bag of groceries in her arms and put two more down on the floor. "There's more," he said, and was out the door, jogging back to his car.

Monica leaned weakly against the doorjamb and followed him hungrily with her eyes. He was wearing his usual three-piece suit, an oxford-cloth shirt, a conservative tie, and wing-tip shoes. He looked the way he always did—devastatingly handsome. Suppressing a moan, Monica reeled toward the kitchen, burying her nose in the sweet-smelling roses, realizing that her work was cut out for her.

When Marc staggered into the kitchen under a barrage of grocery bags, Monica was standing at the sink, carefully arranging the roses in a tall crystal vase. Marc dropped the bags on the table and came up behind her, put his arms around her waist, and drew her back against him.

Monica took a deep breath and tried to combat the wave of pleasure that surged through her. Dammit, he wasn't playing fair! He was using every piece in his arsenal to totally devastate her defenses.

"Hungry?" he murmured, nibbling at her ear.

A delicious spiral swirled in her midsection, and before she knew it she was turning into his arms, sliding her arms around his neck and lifting her lips to his. "Mmm," she murmured, giving herself up to the pleasure of his kisses. "Very."

Her response seemed to ignite his ardor. Suddenly his kisses were more demanding, his tongue more eager, his arms tighter around her, while his hands ran up and down her back in barely controlled desire. He pressed her against the sink and thrust himself against her, making it vividly clear just how aroused he was.

"Marc," she gasped, breaking from him and pushing him away. "What are we having for dinner? Chicken? Veal?" She hurried to the bags he'd deposited on the table and peered into them, pulling out lush green heads of lettuce and late native tomatoes, a bunch of fresh carrots, parsley. "I really am hungry," she said, turning to glance at him.

He was leaning against the counter, his arms folded, one corner of his mouth twisted into a wry grin. "You sure can deflate a man's ego, Monica Bliss," he drawled. "Here I thought you were hungry for me, and it turns out all you're interested in is food."

She shrugged lightly and dragged a bag of apples from another brown grocery bag. "Yum," she said, tearing into the bag and polishing an apple against the sleeve of her sweater. "I love apples." She bit into the apple heartily, then peered into another bag and came to a stop.

"What the . . . ?"

She stepped back as Marc drew a huge bird from the bag. "Duck," he said, dangling the naked bird in the air for her inspection. "Like it?"

"Duck?" she repeated in amazement. "Where do you shop? Or did you take your rifle into the Maine woods just for tonight's dinner?"

He just grinned at her and began to clear out a space for the bird on the shelf of her refrigerator. "Duck *à l'orange* is my speciality," he said, looking back at her from the refrigerator, "but I can do a currant sauce or wild blueberry sauce too. Name your pleasure."

"À l'orange, by all means," she said, amazement making her voice weak. "Do you do this sort of thing for all your women?"

He came to a stop just in front of her. "Only for the future mother of my children," he murmured.

Shocked, she simply stared at him, then backed away. "No, Marc. Child. I only want one child, and it will be mine, not yours. That's part of the agreement."

"Well, you might get more than you bargained for. I hear twins run in my family."

She frowned. "In the English family? That's strange. I didn't know that. I know your cousin Emily and your aunt and uncle and from what I've heard, there've never been twins."

He shrugged off her words and pulled a bottle of white wine from one bag and a wedge of Brie and some Edam from another. "There are crackers and green and red grapes over there. Could you put them out while I get the duck in the oven?"

"Hey," she teased. "I thought you were in charge of this meal. You mean you expect me to do something? I'd planned to give myself a pedicure and soak in my tub while you slaved downstairs in the kitchen."

"Oh, all right," he said with mock exasperation. "Go on and soak, but save a little hot water for me, will you? I plan on taking a shower and shaving before this elegant meal."

She shook her head wonderingly. "You really are something. You're going all out, aren't you?"

He took out a package of wild rice and hefted it in his hand. "I have a philosophy, Monica—if you're going to do something, do it well. Lawyering, cooking, or making babies—I do them all with equal expertise."

Monica felt a strange thrill go through her at his words. Suddenly they were treading on dangerous ground, but she liked it, enjoying the erotic flavor that lay in the air between them. "Have you made many babies before, Mr. English?" she asked.

"No babies," he said, his voice low and husky, his eyes holding hers with their intensity, "but I've had occasion to practice for the procedure. I don't think you'd be disappointed in my performance."

It was a challenge and a promise at the same time, and Monica didn't know how to respond. Part of her wanted to take him by the hand and lead him upstairs to bed and urge him to prove it, but a saner part cautioned her to take care, lest she lose her head and commit a grievous error.

"Cook your goose, Marc, or whatever it is," she said dryly. "And worry about how you perform for a petrie dish." With that, she turned and walked out of the kitchen. Halfway upstairs, it hit her that she might have had the last word, but Marc just might get the last laugh.

Six

Monica was breast-high in bubbles when the first cooking odors permeated her upstairs bathroom. At first she thought her lavender bubblebath had transformed itself into oranges, then she realized she was smelling the orange sauce for the roast duck. Smiling dreamily, she lay back in her massive tub and lazily slathered a fat, soapy sponge over her silken thigh.

If Marc were planning a romantic supper, she couldn't very well appear dressed in her usual home attire. She decided to wear her pale rose crepe blouse paired with loose crepe lounging pants and pink velvet ballet slippers. The blouse had tiny fabric-covered buttons that marched down the front. The more buttons left undone, the sexier the blouse became. Sighing, Monica decided she'd better leave it buttoned all the way to the neck. She couldn't risk turning Marc on. As it was, she'd need all the strength she could muster to resist him.

Somehow, though, when she was out of the tub and smelling like lavender, she couldn't bring herself to button her blouse all the way to the neck. She settled on leaving the top buttons undone so that there was just a hint of décolletage, then she put a dab of perfume on her wrists and at the pulse in the hollow of her throat, and stood back.

Her platinum hair swept back from her high forehead, falling to just above her shoulders in its usual elegantly simple style. She wore pearls, but no other jewelry. Her eyes seemed bluer tonight, her cheeks more pink, her lips more lustrous. There was a softness about her that hadn't been noticeable in years, and she felt excited and wary, hopeful and scared at the same time.

Then she heard whistling and the sound of footsteps ascending the staircase, and she turned off her light and left the bedroom. She stood at the top of the staircase, watching as Marc slowly came toward her. He had a soft-sided suit-bag slung over his shoulder and a small leather shaving kit in one hand. His hair was mussed and the top buttons of his shirt were undone, giving her the first glimpse of his chest.

It was a magnificent chest, she decided, based on what little she saw of it. His neck was as tan as his face, and a few wisps of dark hair hinted at the cloud that probably covered his muscular body. Standing at the top of the stairs, watching him climb slowly toward her, Monica had to put a slim hand on the banister to steady herself.

At the third step from the top, Marc saw her and came to a halt. He let his eyes sweep slowly over her from head to toe then he met her gaze. "You look beautiful," he said, his voice sounding unusually husky.

"Thank you." She stared into his eyes, feeling nervous and exhilarated at the same time, yet determined to resist his advances. Sleeping with Marc might be a woman's dream, but getting involved with him could turn into a nightmare.

There was enough discussion in the media about the problems that arose when people tried to have children out of the normal context of marriage. Wherever legal contracts were involved, problems could arise. No one knew that better than Monica.

She'd therefore have to keep this relationship a business one. It was the only safe way. Having her own child was too important to jeopardize because of an ephemeral physical attraction that would be assuaged in one night. She turned on her heel and spoke over her shoulder, her voice the professional one she used in court.

"You can shower and shave in the guest room," she said, opening a door and standing back to allow Marc to enter.

Instead of going past her, he stopped next to her, sending a flock of butterflies scattering in all directions in her stomach. He smelled of a combination of that devastating aftershave, oranges, and beer.

Her nose wrinkled. "Where did you find beer?" she asked, surprised. "I don't keep any in the house."

"I brought it with me," he said, leaning against the doorjamb, his suit-bag still dangling over his shoulder. "A man's got to be prepared for any and all circumstances."

He was purposely baiting her. She leaned back against the opposite doorjamb and folded her arms, her expression ironic. "It won't work, Marc," she said dryly. "I'm immune to you. I was vaccinated two years ago."

His eyes slowly traveled from her eyes to her lips, then down to the bare skin exposed in the opening of her blouse. "However, I'm happy to say I'm not immune to you," he said in that slow, hypnotizing voice that sent shivers over her entire body. "Some women pall. You see them at first and they intrigue you, but the more you're with them, the less you're interested. But you're not like that. Your looks attract a man at first, but something deeper than appearances keeps him interested. You're like a drug, Monica. You get in a man's system. You make him want you all the time, night and day." He tilted his head, his gray eyes smoky with sensuality, his voice low and husky. "Gets to be a man can't sleep from thinking about you."

Monica stared at him, feeling all her well-laid plans begin to crumble. Her body was no longer in her control. Instead, she was feeling weak and nerveless. Her knees were wobbly, her stomach was churning with desire, and her breathing was shallow, and if Marc didn't stop talking this way she'd grab his hand and haul him over to that bed and rip his clothes off. She would keep him here a week, two weeks, a month—doing all those outlandish things he'd fantasized about and more. She would cover him with kisses, explore that beautiful muscular body with her tongue, her lips, her hands....

Taking an unsteady breath, she launched herself blindly into the guest room. "There's a bathroom through here," she said, talking too fast. She flung open the linen closet door. "Here. Towels, as many as you want." She slammed the door and flung open the medicine cabinet. "Soap. Toothpaste. Disposable razors." She rammed the door shut and tore back the shower curtain. "Hot water, but I recommend cold." For the first time, she met his gaze, and realized he could see right through her. "In fact, I'll bring up a tray of ice," she said, backing from the bathroom, her eyes not leaving Marc. "Maybe that'll keep the animal in you at bay, Mr. English."

"If there's any animal in me, Monica," he said softly, "it's because I sense animal in you."

She turned on her heel and stalked across the room. "Don't fool yourself, Marc. This is Monica Bliss you're talking to, ice maiden extraordinaire." At the door, she'd recovered her poise well enough to look back and make a final parry. "I do recommend you cool it, Marc," she purred. "I'd hate to see you get hurt." With that she closed the door gently, then collapsed against the wall. Oh brother, things were bad and rapidly getting worse. If she wasn't careful, Marc would end up staying the night.

Feeling shaky, she pushed away from the wall, and went downstairs. She was halfway down when she heard soft, sexy blues playing on the stereo system. She frowned and entered the living room. He'd obviously brought his own albums, for she didn't have any that sounded that sexy. He'd also lit a fire in the fireplace and set out champagne in a silver ice bucket. Two crystal flutes sat on a silver tray next to the champagne, obviously waiting for a romantic toast. Sighing, she wandered toward the dining room and came to a stop in the doorway.

Marc had struck again. The table was set with bone china, complete with sterling silver flatware, crystal wine and water goblets, and the roses he'd brought earlier. White tapers were set in silver candlesticks, ready to be lit. Monica slumped against the door and stared at the romantic setting. After two nights of reconnaissance, Marc had brought out the big guns. The war was on.

Monica touched her champagne flute to Marc's, laughing softly. He was delightful company—attentive, amusing, gentlemanly, informed, intelligent. She wrinkled her nose at the scintillating bubbles that tickled her nose and sipped the dry champagne, her eyes dreamy as she stared at the crackling fire. Somehow, she'd gotten to liking the slow, sexy blues music that played in the background. It didn't bother her any more that Marc had turned off all but one lamp in a far corner, which cast only a dim, golden pool of light that barely illumined the room. She liked the way the firelight reflected shadows off the walls, liked the way her feet were curled beneath her on her large ivory cushioned couch, her pink ballet slippers kicked off, her muscles relaxed, her mind at ease.

She had to face it; she liked everything about tonight, particularly Marc. He'd showered and shaved, then changed into an elegant black dinner jacket, slacks and white shirt. With his tan face, gray eyes, and dark hair, he might have been a male model who had just stepped from the glossy pages of an upscale magazine.

He'd taken a seat on the floor near her, so that his elbow rested on the couch cushions not far from her thighs. She sat on the couch and gazed down at the dark red highlights that shimmered in his hair in the firelight, and felt a strange shiver go through her. He hadn't tried anything, hadn't been in the least suggestive, was, in fact, a perfect gentleman all through the delicious dinner.

Now they were finishing their champagne in front of the fireplace, listening to soft, sexy music, both of them relaxed and comfortable. Marc had kept her enchanted with a series of ridiculously funny stories about working with Smitty, then somehow the talk had switched to his family. She sat now, her chin cupped in her hand, her eyes filled with warmth as she listened to him relate a story about family vacations on Block Island when he was a boy.

"It sounds like a dream," she said when he lapsed into silence. "Clambakes and bonfires on the beach and midnight skinny-dipping." She sighed wistfully. "I never did anything like that. I was too busy upholding the family honor. After my mother died when I was thirteen, I went to a horrible girls' camp every summer. I hated it. We played volleyball and field hockey and rode horses." She paused. "Well, actually, I liked the horses. They were great."

"What about boys?"

She laughed lightly. "Oh, come on, Marc. I had my first date when I invited Mike Van Patten to my senior ball at boarding school."

"I didn't know you went out with Mike."

"I didn't. We went to that one dance and never looked at each other again. He met Marcy that night and married her right after college."

"Did you have a crush on him?"

"I had a crush on anything in pants," Monica said, laughing. "Girls who are isolated from boys tend to build castles in the air about anything that walks by. I liked Mike, then Peter Crenshaw, then, let's see..." She began ticking names off her fingers. "Oliver Inman, Greg Tillotson, Jeffrey Lichtman—" She smiled sarcastically. "But eventually my father called me into the drawing room after a date, sat me down and discussed how proper people were more selective and only dated in their own class."

"What happened?"

"I shocked myself, actually. I got pretty mad and called him a narrow-minded, intolerant, mean-spirited bigot."

"How old were you?" Marc asked.

"Let's see, that was during my freshman year, I think, so I'd have been eighteen."

"So you stood up to him."

Monica stared into the fireplace, then met Marc's gaze. "No, that was Monica's last stand, I'm afraid. He pulled me out of Penn State and sent me to Smith. That was his idea of punishing me."

"So any sort of rebellion by you was doomed to failure. You were punished immediately."

She shrugged, tracing her perfectly manicured nail along a crease in her loose crepe trousers. "It wasn't so bad really," she said absently. "I met a boy from Amherst."

The fire crackled and snapped as a log settled, and Marc got up and put another log on, then sat down on the other end of the couch. "And what happened with the boy from Amherst?"

Monica stared unseeingly into the fire as if hypnotized by the flames. "We fell in love," she said softly.

Marc sat watching her, but she wasn't even aware of him. She was remembering Andy, remembering his laughter and smile, remembering how he'd made love to her that first time, all fumbling awkwardness, but gentle, kind, adoring. It was the first time in her life she'd ever felt loved, and it was a revelation. She'd floated through her classes, suspended in a cloud of golden happiness, dreaming of the day they'd graduate and get married.

"I remember the day Andy asked me to marry him," she said out loud, not even knowing she was speaking. "We were holding hands, walking along the Amherst campus, and we stopped under this marvelous old maple tree. The sky was a vivid, electric blue, so bright it almost hurt the eyes, and it was just chilly enough to need sweaters...." Monica closed her eyes and rested her head back against the plush cushions of the couch. "God, I wish life were as simple as I thought it was that day."

"So you said yes to him," Marc said quietly.

She raised her head and stared at him uncomprehendingly. "Yes?"

"When Andy asked you to marry him." He hesitated.

"Oh. Oh, yes," she said, frowning. "Yes, I did. Of course." She rubbed her forehead as if she had a headache, still frowning. "It's too bad," she said absently.

"Too bad you said yes?"

"No. Too bad we didn't get married."

"What happened?"

Without thinking, Monica got up and walked toward the fireplace where she kept a photograph of Amy. "My father intervened," she said, staring at the picture. "I was supposed to go to law school after college, and he said we couldn't get married until I'd finished."

"But you didn't, at least as far as I know."

"No, we didn't."

Marc came up behind her. "She's cute," he said, picking up the photograph. "Who is she?"

Monica went cold, as if all her blood had frozen in her veins. "That's Amy," she said lightly, trying to keep from trembling. "My cousin's little girl."

"Isn't this the same photograph you have on your desk in your office?"

"Is it? Yes, I suppose it is, come to think of it." Turning, she walked toward the kitchen. "I'll make coffee," she said over her shoulder. "You'll need some before you drive home."

She closed the door to the kitchen and took a steadying breath. The earlier mood of camaraderie had been destroyed. How had he gotten her to talk about the past like that? My God, she'd even mentioned Andy. And then to have him ask about Amy's photograph.... She'd have to be even more careful from now on. Without even knowing it, she was beginning to tell Marc things she'd never told anyone in her life, things she hadn't thought about for years.

Rubbing her hands together nervously, Monica tried to remember why she was in the kitchen. Oh, yes, she was going to make coffee. But before she could begin, the door opened and Marc strode in, carrying the dripping ice bucket and empty champagne bottle.

"I told you I'd cook tonight and that includes making coffee at the end of the evening. Unfortunately," he said, taking her by the hand and pulling her back to the living room, "it's not the end of the evening."

"Marc!" she protested, but he silenced her and indicated the chess board he'd set up on the coffee table in front of the fireplace.

"Chess!" she said, irritably. "I'm not in the mood for games, Marc. I'm ready for bed." He looked up, one brow cocked inquiringly. She tilted her head to the side and gave him a disparaging look. "I meant I was ready for you to go home so I could go to bed. Alone. We're going to Vermont tomorrow, in case you've forgotten.''

"Tomorrow?''

"I always go up on Friday afternoon. I leave work early to beat the traffic. Of course if you can't take off early, I'll understand,'' she said lightly. "I don't mind spending the weekend alone in Vermont. I do it all the time.''

"That's not part of our agreement,'' Marc pointed out.

She shrugged and began toying with the chess pieces. "I know you probably can't take off from work as easily as I can, but I'm not going to stick around here Friday night and leave Saturday just to make it convenient for you. You either come up with me tomorrow afternoon, or you don't go at all.''

"I could always join you on Saturday.''

"I suppose. But I'd be long gone, scouring the country-side for antiques. You'd have a long wait sitting on the doorstep.'' She smiled devilishly, thinking of Marc in a three-piece suit, stuck on her front porch all day. "You could always commune with nature, I suppose.''

"I'll leave with you tomorrow,'' he said.

"Oh.''

"You sound disappointed.''

"Not in the least,'' she said. "Meet me at my office at noon and we can get a nice early start. We'll be up there by two-thirty or three.'' She frowned. "Let's see now. I can never remember, which way do knights move? At right angles? Or is that bishops? The queen can move any way, I know. Or is that the king? It's been a long time since I've played this game and—'' Suddenly she stopped talking. Marc had silently gotten up and sat down beside her. His broad shoulder brushed hers, and he was caressing her with his eyes.

She took a deep breath and felt nervous flutters ripple through her body. "What are you doing?" she asked breathlessly.

"You're wondering how the chessmen move. I thought it would be easier to show you from here."

He was lying, she knew that much. From the look on his face, he seemed more interested in making a move of his own on her. She shifted on the cushion, then realized too late he'd set it up so she was wedged between the couch and the coffee table. There was no way out, save over Marc, and she wasn't about to get near the man.

She watched apprehensively as he picked up a bishop and hefted it in his hand. "The bishop," he said in that low, hypnotic voice, "moves diagonally." He reached out and traced a fingertip diagonally across the exposed skin just beneath her pearls. "Like this."

She began to tremble. His fingertip barely touched her skin, but it seemed as potent as a torch, searing her skin with its imprint.

"The knight," he said, "moves at right angles, like this." He moved his finger down almost to the shadow where her breasts swelled, then moved horizontally to the right, tracing the sweet swell of the top of her left breast, coming to a stop at the silky edge of her blouse.

She swallowed, her pulse suddenly hammering, her ears filled with its thunder. She felt her nipples begin to harden into arousal, felt the long, slow spiral of desire begin in her midsection. Suddenly she was dissolving into softness, forgetting all injunctions against enjoying this man. She gazed at his lips and felt her own lips part in expectation, felt her entire body melt toward him as he moved his hand sensuously up and around her neck to cup her head and tilt it back for his kisses.

But he didn't kiss her. Instead he rubbed his thumb over the soft skin just beneath her ear, his eyes holding hers with their intensity. "I've been thinking about this moment all night long," he murmured. "Ever since you opened the front door and I kissed you and you kissed me back. Ever since in the kitchen, when I stood behind you and put my arms around you, and you turned around and put your arms around me and kissed me so hungrily."

He moved his hand down her back and began to brush soft kisses over the skin his thumb had just sensitized. "Your body against mine felt so right, Monica, so good. I keep imagining holding you without any barriers, without silky blouses and lacy bras in the way, without ties and starched shirts." His breath feathered over her skin, sending her into a spasm of longing.

"I've been thinking about it all week, lying in bed at night, unable to sleep, picturing us together, seeing you with me, caressing me, touching me..."

"Oh, Marc," she breathed shakily. "No..."

"Yes," he whispered, dropping feathery soft kisses on her lips. "Yes," he said again, then spoke in a low, hypnotic voice. "When people make love for the first time, it's like an explosion, don't you think?" He didn't allow her to respond. "The need builds up, and the attraction sizzles just under the surface, and pretty soon they can't be with each other without thinking about it, without envisioning what it would be like together. Isn't it that way for you? Don't you look at me and see yourself unbuttoning my shirt, touching me, kissing me?"

"Oh, Marc," she breathed raggedly, beginning to kiss him with fierce, hot kisses. "Don't talk so much. Hold me. Touch me."

"Where do you want me to touch you?" he murmured, his mouth moving hungrily over hers as he lay her back against the cushions.

"Everywhere," she said shakily. "Touch me everywhere. Kiss me all over." She pulled on his tie and loosened it, unbuttoned his shirt, then slid her hands inside and gasped at the tactile pleasure of his warm skin under her hands.

He pulled his shirt out of his trousers and it fell open to reveal a sculpted, muscled chest covered with a cloud of soft black hair. Ridges of muscles scalloped his midriff, and his skin was warm and firm, the color of golden sand on a moonlit beach. She ran her hand down his stomach to the waistband of his trousers, then up again, glorying in the rippling muscles, the texture of his skin, the heat that emanated from it, the fine tickling warmth of the hairs that sprinkled his chest. She ran her fingertips around his nipples and shivered at the way they blossomed under her touch.

"Kiss me there," he groaned, his tongue flicking like heated lashes into her ear.

Trembling, she dropped soft kisses along the strong column of his neck, down into the warm cloud of hair, then over the swell of muscle to the pale tan nipple that stood erect, waiting for her touch. "I didn't know men liked to be kissed there," she whispered.

He groaned and put his arms around her, pulling her down on top of him. "Honey," he said on an almost painful laugh, "men like to be kissed everywhere."

"Just like women," she said.

He stared up at her, then ran his hands into her hair, holding her head while he gazed into her eyes. "Do you want me to kiss you?"

She began to shake inside, growing hot, filled with an ache she couldn't assuage. "Yes," she whispered. "Yes, I do." She bent to him then, caressing his nipples with her lips and tongue, then shuddering as he moved his hands up her body and cupped her breasts.

Her breath came out on what seemed to be an explosive sigh, yet she knew it was barely a whisper in the quiet of the room broken only by the crackling of the fire and their tormented breathing. Slowly he began to unfasten her blouse, slipping his hands inside, cupping her breasts, tormenting her as his thumbs brushed erotically back and forth over her swollen nipples. When she thought she would scream from desire, he unclasped her bra and it fell off, freeing her breasts which spilled into his waiting hands.

She gasped in ecstasy, moving her body back and forth over his chest, rubbing her breasts against his loving palms, glorying in the wildfire of his touch. Then he took her nipple into his mouth, drawing it in with his lips and tongue and laving it in erotic circles until she began to tremble. Suddenly he rolled her over so she was on her back and he atop her.

She wrapped her arms around him and gave herself up to the glorious music that filled her. Her mind ceased to function, and she became all feeling as he scraped his thumb back and forth over one swollen nipple while his lips and tongue teased the other. She felt as if she were drowning in the sensations that shook her body, yet she was vividly aware of his weight atop her, of the intimate closeness of their bodies, of the imprint his hardened manhood made against her.

Suddenly Marc sat back, his legs on either side of her body. Slowly he ran his open palms down her chest, then up again to cup her breasts, the entire time his eyes holding hers, not letting her look away.

"You're as beautiful as I always dreamed," he said. "As warm and responsive as I'd hoped." He continued to caress her breasts as he spoke. "If I were smart, I'd pick you up and carry you upstairs and make love to you all night, but I want to be certain it's what you really want. I don't have any doubts, Monica—I never have had doubts about you. I've wanted you from the very first time I saw you.

"But what you're planning is so important, so frightening a change in both our lives, that I'm going to slow down before things get any further out of hand. I may kick myself all over when I walk out that front door, but I can't risk taking you to bed when it might be the champagne and roses working, not me. Do you understand that I'm leaving because I want you to be sure?"

She took a deep breath and nodded. When he stood up, she began to dress with shaking fingers. While he did the same, she sat in front of the fireplace staring at the flames, her chin cupped in her hand. She was in control again, and desperately grateful for what Marc had just done. She wouldn't have been able to stop, wouldn't have wanted to. The heat of passion had clouded her thinking, deposed all reason, and made her a prisoner of desire.

For the first time she realized what she was involved in, and was badly frightened. She wanted a baby, yes, but she had to be extremely careful. Unthinking indulgence in passion could mean making a mistake. A blunder now could backfire a few months down the road. If Marc ever discovered what she'd done all those years ago, he might try to take the baby away from her. She had to be cool, had to make sure she'd tied up every loophole.

Tomorrow, before they left for Vermont, she'd examine the document she'd drawn up for Marc to sign and try to spot any flaws. Then she'd ask him to sign it before they even went to Vermont. That way, if something happened and she couldn't stay out of his bed any longer, she'd be safe.

But she would stay out of his bed. She had to. She'd already lost one child in her life. She wasn't about to lose another.

Seven

When Marc arrived at her office the next day, Monica had changed into tan corduroy trousers and a heather blue crewneck sweater, but she hadn't changed her professional demeanor. She held out a new copy of the agreement to Marc. "Sign it," she said, "or I'm not going on with this farce."

"You'd go back on an agreement?"

"You're darned right I would," she said cheerfully. "Sign it, please."

Marc rested a muscular thigh on her desktop and folded his arms, looking complacent and amused. "This must mean I'm getting to you, Monica. You must be pretty worried that you'll end up in bed with me this weekend, or you wouldn't be so worried about my signing this."

"Don't push your luck, Marc," she warned. "I'm not in a very good mood today."

"No? Why not? You were pretty loving last night."

"Which is probably why I'm not in a good mood today," she countered. "I always regret it when I make a mistake."

"You call last night a mistake?"

She nodded. "A big one." She handed him a pen and smiled sweetly. "Now sign on the dotted line like a good boy, hmm?"

His eyes glittered with amusement, but he took the pen and Monica called in Terry to witness his signature. She took a relieved breath when he'd signed. It was like taking out an insurance policy—she suddenly felt safer. Now if by chance she slipped this weekend and fell into Marc's arms, she'd be covered in case she got pregnant. Actually, the next few days wouldn't be a bad time—by her calculations, she should be at her most fertile.

She smiled at Terry, told her to take the afternoon off and enjoy her weekend, then looked back at Marc and felt her heart stop. He was looking at Amy's picture again.

"She's a cute little girl," he said, looking up at Monica.

She stared at him, feeling cold all over yet knowing she had nothing to worry about. If she acted guilty, he'd think something was wrong. She forced herself to nod unconcernedly, then picked up her suitcase and looked over her shoulder. "Coming?"

Marc frowned thoughtfully, looking from her to the photograph, then he slid off the desk. "You driving?" he asked.

"Why not? My car almost knows the way by itself. Why don't you drive over to my condo and put your car in my garage, and I'll meet you there."

Fifteen minutes later, Marc stowed his bag in the trunk of Monica's car and climbed in the front seat next to her. "You go up to Vermont every weekend?" he asked as she guided the car onto the back road that would take them toward the northbound interstate.

"Not every one, but quite often, especially in the summer and fall. Spring's not too great up there—it's all mud and bugs—and I'm not a great skier, though I do go up occasionally in the winter for the peace and solitude."

"Don't you ever get lonely up there by yourself?"

"Sometimes," she admitted. "But I keep pretty busy. I try to do my own repairs on the cabin, and I go out antiquing, and I take walks. At times I wish I had a companion—a dog maybe, but somehow I come home and hit the office and I'm so busy I don't see daylight until the next Friday afternoon, and then it's too late to worry about getting a dog."

"What about a man?" Marc asked.

She didn't respond right away. She supposed Marc had a right to know why she felt the way she did, but she'd still have to be careful what she told him. "There's only been one important man in my life, Marc. I didn't marry him because my father wanted me to finish school first, and later...well, it just didn't work out. I guess now I'm so used to being on my own that love is the farthest thing from my mind."

"Don't you ever have cravings for affection?"

"That's none of your business," she said coolly.

"It sure seemed like my business last night."

"Last night was sex," she said irritably. "It didn't have anything to do with love."

"So you admit it was good last night."

"Oh, for heaven's sake, Marc," she said, "it was terrific, okay? It was stupendous. My lord, remind me never to go all the way with you. You're probably one of those men who asks how it was afterward."

"What's wrong with that?" he asked innocently.

She threw him a disgusted look. "Come off it. The man who asks how it was isn't asking because he cares about the woman, he's asking because he cares about himself. It's narcissistic."

Marc was silent a moment, then began to chuckle lazily. "But all this doesn't explain why you have this aversion to marrying now," Marc said. "I mean, if you want a child, why not go the usual route and get married? Surely you don't believe all those surveys that say a single woman in her thirties has almost no chance of finding a mate."

"Good heavens no. I suppose it has to do with my parents' marriage," she said slowly. "It was unhappy, to say the least. There was no warmth, no affection, no sharing. My father worked seventy or eighty hours a week, and my mother drank and went to social functions. We weren't a family, we were a co-op. We lived together, but there wasn't any love that held us together."

"You sound as if you think that just because your parents' marriage was that way, yours would have to be."

"Wouldn't it?" she asked. "They're my role models, after all. If a child doesn't learn about love from her parents, who does she learn from?"

"Yet you want a child," Marc said slowly. "If I remember correctly, you said you want to love it, to give it everything you didn't have. If your reasoning made sense, you wouldn't know how to love it because you feel you weren't loved as a child."

She frowned. It was obvious he was finding a lot of holes in her logic. But what else could she say? She couldn't tell him she was afraid to marry because she thought she'd never find a man who could understand what she'd done when she was nineteen. What man would want that kind of weak, spineless woman for a wife?

"It seems to me that if you can love a child," Marc continued, "you can love a man. And loving a man might just be a lot healthier. I've run into a few women in my time who've devoted themselves solely to their children, and they end up doing more harm than good. A woman is meant to love a man, Monica, and one result of that love is a child. Why are you refusing to let yourself have it all? Why are you allowing yourself only half a life?''

"I can't believe you!" she cried. "You're a fossil! This is the latter half of the twentieth century, for heaven's sake! Women are raising children by themselves, they're becoming surrogate mothers, they're using sperm banks. Honestly, Marc, if I didn't know you were educated, I'd fear you were benighted. You sound like a male chauvinist who thinks a woman has to be barefoot, pregnant, and *married* to find any meaning in life.''

"No, I don't think that at all. I think that men *and* women need each other. It's a two-way street. I don't think my life as a forty-one-year-old bachelor is any healthier than your life as a thirty-five-year-old single woman.''

"Well, at least you didn't call me a spinster," she said ironically.

"The point is, Monica, that there's no reason why you should give up on marriage. Your marriage wouldn't have to automatically be a failure just because your parents' marriage was. You also wouldn't have to necessarily give up your career. Men *are* slowly becoming more enlightened. We're beginning to realize that women need work as much as we do.''

"And do men need love as much as women presumably do?'' she asked ironically. Actually, she was almost enjoying this conversation. If she didn't know better, she'd think Marc was making a pitch to marry her himself!

"What do you mean?''

"Oh, Marc, you sound just like the guy who tries to convince everyone he's not prejudiced by saying he has friends who are black. A woman's work shouldn't even be part of the conversation. A man's isn't. It's assumed a man will work. It's *considered* that a woman may continue to work.

The question is always there—will she stop working when she has kids?'' Monica shook her head. ''I may have become a lawyer to please my father, but I've found out I'm a damned good one—it must run in the genes—and as much as I want a child, I want to work, too.

''But your attitude is one of the reasons I'm reluctant to think about marriage in the first place. I'm afraid men just *say* they understand about a woman's need to work. After he's married a while and things begin to pall a little, wouldn't all the man's inborn prejudices start showing up?''

''Inborn prejudices?'' Marc sat up, his eyes disbelieving.

''You heard me.''

''And what about women's inborn prejudices?''

''We don't have any,'' she said, laughing. ''Oh, lighten up, Marc. You'll spoil a perfectly wonderful weekend.''

He stared at her, then harrumphed, folded his arms again and promptly went to sleep.

''Wake up, sleepyhead,'' Monica said two hours later. ''We're almost there.''

Marc stirred, but didn't open his eyes. Monica glanced at him and found herself smiling. She liked the idea that he was comfortable enough with her to fall asleep while she drove. It made their relationship seem more friendly and trusting, not just sexual. She reached out and shook him gently.

''Hey, Attorney English,'' she said. ''Court's in session.''

''Le' me alone,'' Marc growled.

She laughed musically. ''You old grump. Come on, wake up. We're almost at the turnoff to my cabin. It's beautiful, Marc. I want you to see it.''

''Why?'' he asked, opening one eye and glaring at her. ''What the hell does it matter if your sperm donor likes the Vermont woods?''

She laughed even more and pointed up ahead. "Look, this is the beginning of my property."

Groaning, Marc sat up and peered outside. Behind ancient stone walls, rolling green fields fell away to a stretch of brilliant maple and oak trees and evergreens. A brook ran alongside the road in front of the stone wall, gurgling over rocks and splashing over fallen logs. Tall maples lined the road on both sides, their branches forming a colorful canopy overhead. Now, in late October, the height of southern Vermont's color had passed, but a few leaves remained on the trees. Most lay on the road and fields, a golden and scarlet carpet.

Monica slowed and turned into a dirt road that snaked into the dense underbrush of trees and evergreens. "My cabin's about a half mile into the woods," she explained. "I have two hundred acres, and no one lives for miles around. It's really private."

"You're really taking me to a love nest, aren't you?" Marc asked.

She threw him an amused look. "Don't you wish."

"Yup. I do. I bet you do, too."

"Don't bet, you'd lose." She maneuvered the car around a bend and suddenly the underbrush fell away and they coasted into a clearing where a log cabin dozed peacefully in the sun.

"Don't you get scared out here all alone?" Marc asked as she pulled the car up in front of it.

"Nope." She got out and retrieved her suitcase and strode toward the door.

Marc got his suitcase and fell in beside her. "I get it. You're trying to impress me with your self-sufficiency, right?"

At the steps that led to the covered porch, she turned to Marc. "I'm not trying to impress you with anything," she said. "If you hadn't invited yourself along this weekend,

you wouldn't have known anything about this place."
Turning on her heel, she ascended the low steps and unlocked the front door.

Marc followed her into the living room, a surprisingly
large room with a huge fieldstone fireplace that took up one
wall. A woodstove mounted on a hearth was on the opposite side of the room. In between, there was a large, lumpy
couch with a long harvest table in back of it, piled high with
magazines and books. Wooden shutters covered the entire
back wall of windows. As Marc looked around, Monica
began opening and folding the shutters back. Slowly the
room came alive with light.

"It's great," Marc said, looking around at the bare wood
floors and the tiny galley kitchen off to the side. "Where do
we sleep?"

"*You* sleep in the loft," she said, pointing up. She jerked
her thumb backward, indicating a closed door off to the
side. "I sleep in there. Alone." She pointed to another
closed door. "The bathroom's there. We'll have to share it,
I'm afraid."

She looked Marc up and down. In this three-piece suit he
looked about as comfortable in her rustic cabin as a hen
looked in a lake. "Oh, Marc," she said, shaking her head
almost ruefully, "you're just not going to fit in."

"I'm not?"

"You're not. There are sheets upstairs. I'm afraid you'll
have to make your own bed." With that, she dusted off her
hands, picked up her suitcase, and disappeared into her
bedroom. As she unpacked, she listened to Marc climb the
clanking iron steps of the circular staircase that led up to the
loft, then heard the floorboards overhead squeak under his
weight.

It wasn't fair of her to do this to him, she thought as she
opened the windows and made her bed, but it was exactly
what she needed to defuse his potent attraction. In a so-

phisticated restaurant or at the symphony or a play in
Hartford, Marc was in his element. He was well dressed,
well mannered, in complete control. In the backwoods of
Vermont, he was bound to lose his edge. He would look
awkward, even foolish perhaps. It was the surest, safest way
she knew to demystify him, make him smaller than life
rather than larger.

Still, as she went outside and began to gather late-
blooming chrysanthemums from the garden, she regretted
having him topple from his pedestal so soon. She'd actually enjoyed the past few days. It was too bad they had to
end, but it was infinitely safer this way. She might not get to
enjoy a tumble in the hay with Marc, but she'd get what she
wanted—in a test tube at the doctor's office. Monica had
learned long ago about delaying gratification; she didn't
settle for transitory pleasures. She set her sights on the future and held out for what she wanted.

She was at the kitchen counter arranging the flowers in an
antique vinegar bottle when she heard Marc's footsteps on
the iron circular stairway. Turning, she almost dropped the
vase when she saw him.

He wore faded, patched jeans that rode low on his lean
hips and molded his muscular legs, and a red-and-black
plaid flannel shirt which had seen so many washings it had
faded into a softness that made her fingers itch to touch it.
On his feet he wore ankle-high workboots of supple, tan
leather, so old and beat-up that he must have had them for
at least a decade.

"You bum," she accused. "You tricked me into thinking
you were a tenderfoot."

"I am," he said, raising his eyebrows and shrugging innocently. "I've hardly ever been to Vermont before."

She folded her arms. "Oh? Where do you wear that stuff?
In New York City at five-star restaurants?"

He rubbed his nose, as much to hide his incipient grin, she decided, as to allay any itch. "Actually, I have a friend who runs a logging camp in Maine. I help him out sometimes."

"Then you must know something about splitting wood."

"A little."

"Good. I've got an entire pile out back. How about making yourself useful this afternoon and splitting some? There's an ax in the woodshed, as well as some wedges."

"You gonna help?"

"I'm going to the store and buy some groceries," she said, depositing the flower arrangement in the center of the antique pine trestle table and fitting her pocketbook over her arm. "See you," she said, dashing out the door.

Standing on the porch, Marc yelled to her, "I thought we were going antiquing."

"That's tomorrow," she yelled back, then grinned to herself as she accelerated in a cloud of dust. Damn Marc English anyway. It was just like him to turn out to be as perfect in jeans as he was in a three-piece suit. Then she frowned, feeling the first inkling that trouble lay ahead. If Marc had been difficult to fight off last night, he'd be that much more difficult to fight off tonight.

They would be alone in an isolated cabin, with a fireplace roaring and oil lamps flickering. They'd share a tiny bathroom with its notoriously recalcitrant hot water heater. And if she did manage to fight him off, she'd lie in bed hearing him toss and turn upstairs on his cot. Could she fight him as well as herself? Lately, her body had been acting headstrong, as if her brain had nothing to do with running things. Unbidden, erotic images would dance into her thoughts, conjuring up all manner of earthy physical delights with Marc.

Driving thoughtfully toward the small country store that served inhabitants of a twenty-mile radius, Monica thought about Andy Emerson. He'd been her first lover. They'd both been awkward and virginal when they first made love, but their passion and love for each other had soon cured that. Her cheeks heated at the memory of how she'd been with Andy—warm, loving, spontaneous, sexy.

It had been a long time since she'd felt any of those things. But now she suddenly felt alive again, and life was once more exciting as well as complicated. Marc had merely to kiss her to cause spontaneous combustion. For the past week, she'd been finding it difficult to concentrate. She was tired at night but unable to fall asleep, and she couldn't chase away the memory of Marc's strong arms around her. And when she did at last manage to fall asleep, she dreamed of him.

She was in trouble. If she didn't watch out, she'd fall for him, and that could be fatal. If Andy hadn't forgiven her for the decision she'd made, how could she expect any other man to understand? Would Marc English?

Probably not. He was the son of a well-to-do family that had never had even a hint of scandal attached to its name. Women didn't have children out of wedlock in the quiet, serene world of the Englishes and their ilk. Everyone was refined, well-bred, and shocked by those who broke the rules.

Not that the rules didn't get broken. Monica almost laughed out loud. She wasn't the only daughter of wealthy parents to find herself unmarried and pregnant. Haunted by her thoughts, Monica pushed open her car door and hurried into the general store. There, the laden wooden shelves and briny odor of pickles and garlic from the deli section chased away her worry. Surrounded by jars of penny candy and boxes of fresh native apples, Monica reaffirmed that any involvement with Marc would be dangerous. She'd have to continue fighting him off, and she'd do it any way she could. If she had to retreat behind a barrier of sarcasm and snide remarks, she would. If she had to repulse his every move, so be it.

She was fighting for something more important than momentary sexual release. She was fighting for the right to her own child. Years earlier, she'd given up that right. Today she wouldn't. Not ever again. No matter what it took, she would have a child, and she'd keep it, and no man on earth would take it from her.

Marc had taken off his shirt and was splitting logs when Monica returned from the store. She pulled her car to a stop and stared at him, swallowing with difficulty around the lump that suddenly lodged in her throat.

He was magnificent—a sweaty, swarthy-skinned man with dark hair on a spectacularly muscled chest, and arms that rippled with sinew and muscle. Her stomach did a slow pirouette and she almost decided to forget her good intentions, then she forced herself to get out of the car, but she still had to fight to keep her knees from buckling.

"Get something good for supper?" Marc called out cheerfully.

"Hard scrapple and sour milk," she snapped, toting two bags of groceries toward the cabin. "And curdled pudding for dessert, if you're lucky."

Marc left the ax wedged in the stump he was using as a chopping block and took off after her, catching up with her at the door to the cabin. "You mad or something?"

She kicked open the door and stalked toward the small kitchen. "Nope."

"Can I help you unpack groceries?"

"Nope." She banged a half gallon of milk on the table and cursed when she almost broke a nail.

"You sure something's not wrong?"

She put her hands on her hips and gave him a long-suffering look. "Nothing is wrong, Marc. I'm busy. I'm not used to company up here and I find I don't like it. If you're smart, you'll go back outside and keep yourself occupied. Please don't bother me."

"That's the problem, isn't it?" Marc said. "I do bother you. Physically."

The room suddenly went quiet. She couldn't look at him, couldn't meet his eyes for fear he'd see the truth in hers. Her senses were screaming with awareness of him, but she had to pretend she was turned off. It was the only way to keep him at a safe distance. She might even have to resort to being downright rude.

She looked him up and down, her face mirroring distaste. "Actually that's true," she said in her most disdainful voice. "You're sweaty and you smell. Is it any wonder I don't find you attractive the way you look?"

She turned away suddenly, knowing she'd found the perfect excuse to keep him at a distance, but inside she was shaking. She hated what she'd just said, hated being cruel to Marc. Her heart felt strangely heavy, and she suddenly felt like crying. But if he knew she wanted to fall into his arms, to feel the marvelous sweaty warmth of his skin against hers, she'd be lost.

But why wasn't he leaving? She turned and found him leaning against the trestle table, his strong arms folded across his chest, looking better than all the pictures of sexy Indian braves she'd ever seen on the lurid covers of historical romances.

"Whether you know it or not," Marc said softly, "I'm exactly what you need."

Her heart stopped beating, then began again on a drumroll. Instinctively she backed away from him, her eyes wide, her lips parted softly. She took an unsteady breath and told herself to keep fighting. Sooner or later he'd give up and go outside and leave her in peace.

He gestured to her immaculate hair. "You see, Monica, you're too perfect. You need a man's hands in your hair, messing it up, a man's smell on your body, mingling with yours. You need to gasp and moan and writhe beneath him, to sweat as much as he does, to rouse up all the womanly smells you've hidden so long under all that exotic perfume you wear."

She stared at him, the blood draining from her cheeks, leaving them pale. "Get out," she whispered. "Get out of here."

Marc continued staring at her. She stared back, unsure if he would leave or advance slowly on her and take her in his arms. If he did, she was truly lost. Slowly, Marc inclined his head, straightened from the table, turned and left the cabin.

Monica let out a trembling breath, then slumped against the wall, her heart hammering painfully, her cheeks suddenly flushed. She must remember not to bait him. It hadn't worked, indeed had backfired badly. She'd have to remember that Marc was a proud man, and would react to any rejection as if it were fuel to his manly flame.

Taking a calming breath, Monica stared at the door. Her only refuge then would have to be cool, disdainful amusement. That was the only weapon she had that he seemed incapable of handling.

Eight

More coffee?'' Monica asked.

"No, thank you,'' Marc responded.

Monica flicked an uneasy look at her houseguest. He was being so egregiously polite, so unerringly well mannered, that she wanted to scream at him to stop the pretense and tell her what he really thought. He had showered and changed into corduroy trousers and a new plaid flannel shirt, but they'd barely spoken two words since their confrontation this afternoon. Now, at the end of a painfully quiet supper of beans and franks and brown bread, he was sipping his coffee from a mug and reading an old copy of *The New Yorker* magazine. Occasionally he would chuckle. She presumed that meant he'd just read one of the cartoons the magazine was famous for.

She cleared her throat. "Would you like to play chess?''

He glanced up and the affability disappeared from his face. "No, thank you," he said coolly, then went back to reading.

Monica shifted uncomfortably in her chair. "How about cards?"

"No, thanks," he said distantly, "but you go ahead. You must play solitaire a lot. I'll bet you're a whiz at it."

"As a matter of fact, I hate the game."

"Do you? Well, that's something we have in common." He went back to the magazine.

She glared at him, then abruptly pushed back her chair and began to clear the table. Ostentatiously, he continued to read the magazine, refusing to look up even when she whisked his plate away.

"Oh, that's okay, Marc," she said with obvious false cheer, "I don't mind cleaning up after you."

He lifted an eyebrow. "If you wanted help, why didn't you ask for it?" he asked.

She shoved the plate onto the counter with a clatter. "I would never dream of asking a guest to help," she said sweetly. "Of course, I'd also never have dreamed there'd be a guest who wouldn't offer. Good ol' Emily Post would be startled out of her knickers—but then, live and learn, I always say."

Marc put down the magazine and stood up. "Your point is abundantly clear, Monica. I'll wash the damn dishes."

"I wouldn't think of having you wash dishes, Marc," she said with even more saccharine in her voice. "Please. Sit down. Put your feet up. It's such a pleasure to have a man around the house. I actually feel like Edith Bunker."

Marc whipped the dishtowel from her hands and began running hot water into a rubberized dishpan. He stared down at it, then frowned. "What's going on? Why isn't the water hot?"

"You want to know why the water isn't hot?" she said, glaring at him. "It's because you stood in the shower for half an hour and used it all, that's why." She filled the kettle and shoved it on the stove. "This is how we'll heat the water tonight. By the morning maybe we'll have enough for both of us, if you can manage to limit your shower to five minutes."

"Do you mean to say there's no hot water?"

"That's exactly what I mean."

"Maybe you should invest a little money in a decent water heater."

"It works just fine for me," she snapped. "The trouble occurs when another person enters the picture."

"That's where all the trouble comes from in your life, isn't it, Monica?"

"What do you mean by that?"

"What do you think I mean?" he snarled, then threw the dishtowel down and stalked toward the front door. "I'm going for a walk. When the damned water's hot, call me and I'll do the damned dishes."

"You don't have to swear so much, Marc," she yelled after him.

"Like hell I don't," he muttered, then tore open the door and slammed it shut after him.

Monica stared after him, then whirled around, putting her back to the door and struggling to keep from crying. The whole weekend was going to be a disaster. Their relationship was in ruins. Everything was a mess, and it was all her fault.

No, it was Marc's fault! If he weren't so determined to sleep with her, they could have had a comfortable friendship and none of this emotional upheaval would have to take place.

Dammit, dammit, *dammit*! No wonder she lived alone! The moment you got mixed up with men and relationships, the roof fell in. She should have known this wouldn't work. You couldn't stick two headstrong people in a small three-room cabin and expect things to go smoothly.

But if he weren't so pigheaded, so obstinate, so—

Monica burst into tears, hugging herself tightly. Who was she kidding? It wasn't Marc's fault; it was hers. She'd been disgustingly rude to him in an effort to keep him from making a move on her. Well, she'd effectively put a stop to any amorous intentions, but she'd also ruined a budding friendship. Why, she'd actually begun to like Marc, to enjoy his company. They'd laughed a lot together, and she'd felt pretty and feminine and desirable...

She brushed away her tears and told herself to stop being such a baby. A grown woman didn't cry over a man. It just wasn't done. She remembered her father scoffing at her when he discovered her crying over Andy Emerson.

"Monica Marie," he'd said, his face as cold as ice, his words as clipped as Marc's had been, "stop that ridiculous crying. You're a woman now, with a great career ahead of you. There's no place for emotion in a court of law."

"What about in a *woman*?" she screamed at him, her eyes red, her face contorted with pain. "What about people, Father?"

He'd merely stared down at her, then he'd turned on his impeccable heel and left her alone there, sobbing. Slowly, her tears had ebbed and she'd straightened those capable shoulders of hers. She was a Bliss, after all, and she was her father's only child. Someday she was going to be a lawyer. Yet why did all that seem so trivial after what she'd given up?

Monica came back to the present with a start. The kettle was whistling. She emptied some of the steaming water into the dishpan, pulled on rubber gloves, and began to wash the dishes, thoughtfully going over the remembered scene in her mind. For sixteen years, she'd lived the life her father had wanted her to lead. She'd graduated from law school at the top of her class, had taken over his practice and established her reputation as a capable and skilled lawyer. She'd denied whole parts of herself to please her father, yet what had it gotten her?

She'd lost touch with her feelings. She'd denied her deepest needs—to love and be loved. She'd become machinelike in her business efficiency, and she'd lost the warmth, spontaneity, and humor necessary to live with others. If only she had it to do over again, she thought, she'd do it differently. She'd refuse to obey her father. She would have married Andy and kept the baby. She still could have gone to law school. Why had she let her father rule her life?

She stared sadly into the past, remembering the young Monica, remembering how she had adored her father. To her, he had been a kind of king—tall, silver-haired, remote. He was always just out of reach, like the Holy Grail, and she had dedicated her life to gaining his love. He'd never made a secret of his disappointment that she wasn't a boy, so she'd worked harder than a son would have worked—studied more, played less. And when the time had come to choose between the man she loved and her father, her father had won. She owed it to him, didn't she? He was her father, after all.

She finished the dishes, dried and put them away, then built a fire in the fireplace and sat in front of it, sipping coffee and staring at the flames, remembering the day she realized what a mistake she'd made. She had just graduated from law school, head of her class, and her father had brought her into her new office and presented her with the portrait of a mother and child.

"It's a Mary Cassatt," he'd said, pride ringing in his voice. "I thought it would make up for Amy." He had paced back and forth, his hands behind his back, his chin high, his

eyes as piercing as any eagle's, and spoken so clearly, so
surely. There was never any room for doubt in her father's
life, never any room for regret.

"That child would have weighed you down, Monica,"
he'd said. "It was the best decision for everyone. Andy
Emerson was a nice boy, but he wasn't for you. He didn't
have the right background. Now this painting," he'd said,
gesturing to the watercolor, "this will appreciate in value.
You'll have something here ten, twenty years from now."

Monica had stared at her father, suddenly seeing him for
what he was, feeling sick at the realization that she'd sold
her soul away as surely as she'd given away her child. She
was as morally bankrupt as her father, as cold and icy as he
was. From that moment, she had hated the portrait and all
it symbolized, but she kept it in her office, looked at it every
day. It was her penance, her payment for giving up what was
dearer than her own life. To please a cynical old man, she'd
spurned Andy's proposal and given up their child. The
contempt in Andy's eyes when he learned what she'd done
was mirrored every day in her own.

How could she ever explain it to Marc and expect him to
understand? How could she expect forgiveness when she
couldn't forgive herself? If she ever told anyone what she'd
done they would hate her as much as she hated herself,
condemn her as much as she condemned herself. She was
trapped with the memory and because of her own weakness
any relationship with a man was doomed. She drew her
knees up and hugged her legs, dropping her forehead to her
knees and closing her eyes on the pain that pervaded her.

If there could be a man, though, if there could be a relationship, she would want it to be with Marc. The trouble
was, there couldn't be. If she stumbled and weakened, giving in to her desire to make love with Marc, she would be
jeopardizing her child's future. The closer she got to Marc,

the more she would want to tell him. She could feel it happening already, could sense her desire to confide in him.

But if she did, she was certain he would try to take the baby from her, and she didn't think she could stand that. She who was outwardly so strong couldn't deal with the loss of another child. This baby would be a way of making reparation for the one she'd given up and would wipe the slate clean and allow her to live with herself. She couldn't let Marc take that away from her.

"You look so unhappy," Marc said quietly from the darkness behind her. "Did our silly spat do that to you?"

Startled, she raised her head and turned toward his voice. He'd come in and closed the door, but she hadn't heard him walk toward her or felt his presence so close behind her in the darkness. She drank him in, feasting her tortured eyes on his face, realizing suddenly how much she cared for him.

She was still paying for her mistake years later, she realized, and the knowledge that once again she'd have to give up someone she loved went through her like a knife.

"It wasn't the fight," she said softly, her voice tinged with sadness and regret. "Not completely anyway." She forced a strangled laugh. "I was just remembering some things from a long time ago, thinking about the past and how we never escape it."

"We *can* escape the past," Marc said, his voice low and almost urgent. "We just have to want to."

She shook her head, turning away from him. "No. Some things can't be escaped, shouldn't be. Some things are too horrible to be forgotten."

"Horrible?" Marc hunkered down beside her, searching her face. "What do you mean? What are you talking about?"

She took a deep breath and shook her head. "Nothing. Did you have a nice walk?"

"I was lonely," he said. "I wished you were with me."

She allowed herself to sink into his eyes, to put all the feeling for him into her own eyes, telling him mutely that she loved him, would never knowingly hurt him, begging him to understand and forgive her for her cruelties. Then she straightened and pulled away, retreated within herself, pulling the cloak of distance around her.

"If I had been, we would have just continued fighting," she said lightly, and stood up, smiling down at him. "I'm going to bed, Marc. See you in the morning."

"You're not going to bed," he said. "You're running away."

She hesitated at the door to her room, faltered, then lifted her chin. "Good night, Marc," she said clearly.

He didn't answer. She began to tremble, wondering if he would get up and come to her, sweep her into his strong arms and take her into the bedroom. She wished he would, wished he would take the responsibility of refusing away from her. It was what they both wanted, but she couldn't allow herself to reach out and take it.

"Good night, Monica."

The words were heavy and final in the dark room. She felt something fall within her, then she walked into her room and closed the door.

She lay awake, listening for Marc to climb the steps to the loft. It was after midnight when he finally did, then she lay stiffly in bed, achingly aware of his footsteps as he moved around overhead. Finally she heard the sound of the bedsprings as he got into the narrow cot. She swallowed thickly, picturing him.

She wondered what he slept in, and if he lay on his back or on his side. Was he awake now, too, listening to the creaking of the cabin, hearing the lonely hoot of an owl, the mournful sound that had frightened her so much when she first stayed here alone? Did he picture her as well, and wonder what she wore? Did his loins burn for her the way hers burned for him? Did his hands ache to touch her, caress her? Did sleep elude him, too?

She sat up and held her head, trying to press out the questions between her palms. She could go to him. She could get out of her bed and climb the winding iron staircase and slip in beside him, turn into his heat and give herself to him. She could lie naked next to him, beneath him, feel his hands and lips and tongue, feel his hot entry penetrating deep into her very soul—

She lay back on her bed, pressing her teeth into her hand to keep from crying out with need. She couldn't think this way, couldn't allow herself to dream these tortured daydreams. She had to sleep. She'd need all her strength to get through the next two days.

"Did you sleep well?" Marc asked over breakfast the next morning.

She glanced at him quickly, then away again. "Yes," she said lightly. "Did you?"

"Not really."

She took a shaky breath and continued spreading butter on her toast. "I'm sorry to hear that. Was it the cot? I know it's narrow. Perhaps you'd be more comfortable on the couch tonight. It's—"

"It wasn't the cot," Marc said, breaking into her nervous chatter. "It was you. You were too close. A dozen times I got up to come to you, and a dozen times I stopped myself."

She swallowed thickly and put the knife down, then picked it up again, then put it down. She wiped her hands on the paper napkin and looked around the room. "It's going to be a nice day. The sky's as clear as a . . ." She shrugged. "The sky's very blue," she finished lamely.

"Did you think about me last night?" Marc asked.

She refused to look at him, refused to respond. "There's a little shop about fifteen miles from here that I want to stop at," she said brightly. "But really, Marc, you don't have to come with me. You can stay here if you like. Take a walk, or a nap—"

"I want to come with you. I want to be with you all the time," he said in that low, hypnotic voice.

It wasn't a morning voice, she thought protestingly. It was a night voice, a voice made for dark places and whispered words. She stood up quickly and took her plate to the sink. "Was there enough hot water for you?"

"There was," he said, "but I didn't need it. Steam was coming off my skin all night. I could have melted an iceberg by this morning."

She pressed her mouth shut tightly, then turned to him slowly. "Look. This is hard for me, too—"

"Is it? Then we can fix that right away. Come to bed with me."

"That's the answer, isn't it, Marc?" she asked sarcastically. "Sex. Good for what ails you." She shook her head and laughed without amusement. "Honestly, if it were up to men, we'd still be living in caves."

"You find my desire for you Neolithic?"

"Neolithic, Paleolithic, whatever. I just wish you'd stop."

"Stop desiring you? Impossible. I've wanted you for years. What really ticks me off, though, is that you're not just fighting me, you're fighting yourself. You want me as much as I want you, yet you're stubbornly refusing to give in. Why? Is it a game with you, Monica? Do you always have to win, to have the upper hand?"

"No!"

"Then what is it?" he demanded. "What the hell kind of demon drives you, Monica? Tell me, dammit."

Shaking, she stared at him, then took a breath and lifted her chin stubbornly. "That little shop has the most amazing collection of thimbles. I seem to remember your saying your mother collects thimbles. Perhaps you'd like to buy her one as a gift.''

A muscle worked agitatedly in his cheek. He stood up and flung down the napkin. ''All right,'' he said. ''I'll play by your rules for now, but tonight, Monica—tonight we play by mine.'' Turning on his heel, Marc strode angrily toward the door.

Nine

Monica stared a moment, then her anger flared and she went after him. She caught up with him at the door. "Wait just a darned minute, Marc English," she said, her voice shaking as she grabbed his arm and spun him around. "Who the hell do you think you are?" she demanded in a throbbing voice. "Where do you get off accusing me of playing games, when all along that's all this is to you? You don't care about me. You don't want me because you love me. You want me because you want me, plain and simple, and whatever the great Marc English wants, the great Marc English gets.

"Well not this time, buddy. I may be an ice maiden to you, but at least I don't hop into just anyone's bed for the fun of it. I need to *care*, Marc, to feel something."

"You do feel something," Marc snarled. "You feel it so bad you're burning up with it. The only trouble is, you've gone so long without any emotion in your life, you can't recognize it even when it hits you in the face." He grabbed her and dragged her to his chest. "Feel it, Monica?" he asked in a low voice. "Feel your heart pounding, your blood turning to fire? That's sex, sure, but it's something else too. Or it could be, if you gave it half a chance." He released her so quickly she stumbled and had to struggle to keep her balance.

"But you're too determined to close yourself off," Marc continued, baiting her. "You're determined to keep a lid on all those emotions that are boiling inside you. It's scary, isn't it, Monica? It's downright frightening, all those feelings just aching to explode. Right now you don't know what to do, do you? You want to hit me and you want to kiss me and you can't figure out which you want more."

He began to walk toward her, forcing her to walk backward, his voice low and filled with something close to contempt, his eyes holding hers, refusing to let her look away. She felt the anger swell inside her in mountainous waves, building and building, soaring inside like a satanic symphony, a cacophony of sound and feeling.

"Well, I'll tell you which you want," Marc went on. "You want to kiss me. You want to dig your nails into my back and tear my clothes off. You want to make love with me, Monica, roll around on that floor with me. You want it so bad you're shaking all over with need. Aren't you?"

His words lay like a challenge in the air between them. For a moment they stared at each other, then she lashed out, slapping him across the face. The sound echoed in the sudden quiet of the room. They stood and stared at each other, stunned by the eruption of anger, then Marc clamped his hands on her shoulders and dragged her into his arms, lowering his mouth savagely to hers and taking her in a fierce kiss that swept away everything but the vital, raw, elemental anger that fueled the hunger between them.

She responded with an ardor that took its strength from all the self-denial of a lifetime. Her need escaped on a rising tide of what at first seemed anger, then revealed itself as desire. She returned his kisses as fiercely as he gave them, pressing her slender body into his, digging her nails into his muscular shoulders, clinging to him, sobbing, letting all the feeling go at last.

His lips scorched her skin, moving down her neck into the sweet valley between her breasts, devouring her with passion as he struggled to undo her buttons. He bent her backward over his strong arm, his lips plundering the sweetness of her skin, his fingers ripping away the buttons that held her blouse closed. At last he buried his face in her breasts, holding her tightly, his chest rising and falling with labored breaths, his arms tight around her.

"I want you," he murmured, unclasping her bra and freeing her breasts for his exploring lips. "I want you," he repeated over and over as his lips devoured her.

She sank with him to the floor in front of the fireplace, running her hands into the thickness of his hair, her face filled with rapture. "I want you, too," she whispered raggedly, covering his face with kisses. "I want you so much, Marc."

As suddenly as it had come, the storm of passion fueled by anger changed, softened, bringing tenderness in its wake. Where Marc's hands had been rough, they became loving, where his kisses had been savage, they became seeking, coaxing. Monica felt herself melting into softness, all the anger burned out of her, leaving only a soaring sensation filling her with aching sweetness.

"Oh, Marc," she whispered, slowly unbuttoning his shirt and sliding her palms over the hair-roughened expanse of his muscular chest. "How could I have been so foolish to think I could stop this?"

"You couldn't have stopped it," he said, running his hand down her back, nuzzling the soft skin just under her ear. "It's too right. It's meant to be, Monica."

Something pure and shining rose up inside her, transforming her face so that she seemed filled with light, radiantly alive. She ran her hands over his back, glorying in the feel of his warm skin beneath her palms, feeling the rising tide of passion return, stronger now, deeper, thrumming inside like a motor, driving her crazy with desire for him.

She unbuckled his belt with shaking fingers, then unzipped his trousers and moved her hands around to his back, sliding her palms inside to grasp his buttocks, holding him tightly to her, reveling in the hardness of his manhood that throbbed against her.

"Make love to me, Marc," she whispered.

He eased her blouse off her shoulders, then dipped his fingers into the waistband of her slacks and panties, dragging them down over the soft swell of her hips, down the long, sleek length of her silken thighs, dropping kisses along them until finally her clothes lay in a puddle on the floor in a patch of sunlight.

He knelt over her, his eyes devouring her. "You're magnificent," he said, running a reverent hand up her calf to the back of her thigh. "All ivory and gold," he murmured, dropping kisses on the inside of her thigh. "Sweet smelling, soft, flawless." His breath whispered over her skin, sending shivers cascading over her as his lips slowly burned an erotic path along her body.

She felt hot, aflame with desire, suspended in some golden land where pleasure mixed with pain. An incessant ache permeated her body, and she sank into the need, falling deeper and deeper, swirling into a land she only dimly remembered, where the body and spirit flowered together in sweet abandon.

Marc pressed soft kisses along her throat and against her breasts. He eased his fingers down her bare thighs, dipping into the core of her, assuaging the hunger for brief seconds, then lifting away, letting the desire return even more strongly until she was trembling, her fingers curled into his hair, her back arched, her head back, her hair flowing behind her like a silver ribbon.

"Oh!" She gasped and fell back, assaulted by a wave of beauty so intense she couldn't move. Her body liquified, transporting her to a different world of golden light and incredible joy. Gasps of pleasure escaped, filling the sunlit room with the music of her desire.

She cried his name, her eyes shut against the blinding radiance, her back arching again as another wave broke over her.

And then he was beside her, holding her in his strong arms as she covered him with kisses. "Oh, Marc," she whispered tremulously, still experiencing the remaining flutters of her ecstatic journey. "That felt incredible," she gasped softly.

"But it's not over," Marc whispered against her lips. "It's just begun."

Slowly she opened her eyes and lay on her side, looking at him. She reached out and ran her finger lightly down his cheek, then traced the outline of his mouth. He opened his mouth and began to suck on her finger, toying with it with his tongue. She felt an answering response deep in her abdomen, a sharp contraction in her muscles as the slow arousal began again.

"How do you turn me on so much?" she whispered, running her fingers down his stomach. She found him hard and pulsing, and lightly traced her fingertips over his heated length, making him groan with need. "How do you make me want you even more than I just did?" she whispered. "How do you make me forget who I am, and turn me into a woman?"

"Like this," he whispered, his lips tracing a blazing path from her neck to her breasts, arousing her nipples to hard peaks.

"And this...." He turned her over and kissed an erotic line down her spine from the nape of her neck to the sweet curve of her waist. She lay on her stomach, shuddering at the feel of his lips and tongue, at the way his hands moved lightly down her sides, along the sleek line of her hips, then down her thighs to her calves while his lips followed with burning kisses.

Hunger took flame, filling her with heat. Turning over, she dragged his trousers and shorts down his muscular legs, dropping kisses along the route, then tossed his clothes on the pile with hers. Slowly, she kissed her way up his right leg, moving her body over his until she lay on top of him, gazing into his eyes.

"You're magnificent," he whispered. "Better than my fantasies."

"What else did I do in your fantasies?" she whispered, rubbing her breasts against his chest. "Tell me. I want to do everything you've ever dreamed about, to be everything you ever wanted in a woman."

He groaned, then his arms were suddenly strong around her and they were rolling together on the floor until she was on her back and he astride her. "I want to fill you," he murmured huskily against her lips, moving himself back and forth over her, filling her with shuddering desire. "I want to enter you and stay in you forever."

Trembling, she returned his ardent kisses, closing her eyes and clasping her arms around him and letting go, floating with him into pleasure so deep, so intense that she forgot everything—her past and the possibility of any future. There was only Marc, driving strongly into her. They were no longer two people, but one, traveling together, linked in an ancient embrace. She felt the glorious heat fill her with a rising tide of passion.

Shivering, she heard her own moans of pleasure as Marc whispered love words in her ear, his voice low and husky, filled with equal measures of pain and ecstasy. His thrusts escalated, became almost fierce, and she clung to him, her hips churning, rising and falling in rhythm with his, until finally he thrust into her so deeply that everything inside her shattered, broke like the sound of millions of angels singing, burst into a billion gold-and-scarlet lights. Beauty such as she had never experienced assaulted her, snatched her into a teeming whirlwind, and flung her into Olympus.

Crying Marc's name, she clasped him closer, tumbling with him into eternity.

Monica lay naked with her head on Marc's chest, gazing at the fireplace. She had no idea what time it was, though night had fallen. She was lost in her dreams, still transported by the lovemaking they had shared all day.

"Are you hungry?" she asked softly.

"Mmm," he murmured, running his hand down her back and up again. He settled his hand around the nape of her neck and tilted her head back to his, kissing her deeply.

"Don't you ever get enough?" she asked, laughing huskily, moving her fingers over his chest.

"Maybe in a few days I will," he acknowledged, nuzzling his nose into the sweet curve where her shoulder met her neck. "Then maybe we can settle down to making love two or three times a day for the next three or four decades. That might keep me satisfied."

She smiled sadly, her cheek resting against his chest again. If only that could happen. "We are good together," she admitted.

"Mmm," he said, fingering the peaks of her breasts into arousal. "We're better than good," he growled into her ear, "we're terrific."

She took a tremulous breath and pushed away. "I think we need to stop a while, though."

"Why?" He followed her as she tried to escape his embrace, pressing kisses in a pathway toward her breasts.

"Because maybe we'll run out of steam," she said, beginning to panic at the way her senses were betraying her.

"I don't think so," he said chuckling. "I don't think that's possible."

"Yes, but . . . we need to take a shower, get dressed, have some supper."

"We do?"

She put a hand against his chest, trying to fight off the dizzying desire that was already assaulting her again. "We do," she said in the firmest tone she could muster.

"Okay," he said, sighing. "If you insist."

"I do," she said, standing up and beginning to gather her clothes. "I need a shower, and so do you. And then something good to eat. Pancakes."

He cocked his head. "Pancakes?" he asked, beginning to look interested. "With maple syrup?"

"Loaded with maple syrup," she said, laughing as she ran for the bathroom. If she got there first, she would lock the door and keep him out, otherwise who knew what would happen. "With great golden puddles of butter and huge, steaming mugs of coffee." She slammed the door, but Marc reached it before she could get it locked. "Marc," she shouted through the door, "I need to shower. You'll just have to wait your turn."

Marc pushed open the door easily. "I've got a better idea. It'll even conserve hot water." He dragged her into his arms and reached out to turn the shower on. "We'll shower together."

"Devil," she whispered.

"Angel," he whispered back as his mouth covered hers.

An hour later, they sat on the floor in front of the fireplace again, their backs resting against the couch, Marc's arm around Monica as they gazed into the flames. For the first time in twelve hours, Monica once again felt in control of her body and her thoughts. She stared unseeingly at the fire, stunned at the sudden realization of what they'd done.

Everything had happened so quickly, so heatedly, that she hadn't once thought about the possibility of having a baby. Babies hadn't even entered into it. Everything had been Marc. Joining with him in loving embrace had been all that mattered, her only motive.

"Marc?"

"Mmm?"

Monica frowned, trying to come to terms with this new and shaking knowledge. "What if I'm already pregnant?"

"That's what you want, isn't it?"

She didn't respond right away. Suddenly she was afraid. The idea of having a child loomed over her like a monster.

"I . . . I don't know," she said. "I guess so. . . ."

"Hey," he said, chuckling, "you sound like you're getting last-minute jitters."

"Don't make fun of me, Marc," she said quietly. "I need to talk and you're the only one here to talk with."

"I'm sorry," Marc said, growing serious. "I wasn't making fun of you. Here." He drew her into his embrace and rested his lips against her hair. "Talk to me. I'm here. I'll listen all you want."

She closed her eyes and hugged him tightly. "I know it's ridiculous," she said, "but it just hit me with a bang all the sudden, the realization that I could be pregnant already. How many times did we make love today? Five? Six? Good grief."

"Do you mean you made love all those times without ever once thinking about having a baby?"

She opened her eyes, realizing she'd told him more than she should have. "I ... well ..." she laughed in confusion. "Well, frankly, Marc, you didn't give me time to think about much of anything."

"Good," he said, his eyes traveling lazily down her body. "Getting you pregnant may take a while, you know, so we may as well enjoy ourselves while we're at it."

"Oh." She sat up, staring wide-eyed into the fireplace. She hadn't thought of that. She'd just supposed that she'd get pregnant right away. But that was foolish of her. "How long do you think it'll take?" she finally asked.

Marc shrugged. "Hard to tell. There's one thing I know from talking with my cousin, though."

"What's that?"

"The more you do it, the better your chances. I think we should plan on meeting every night." He brushed his lips across her shoulder and began to nuzzle her earlobe. "Of course, if you'd prefer it first thing in the morning, I could arrange that. You could give me a key to your condo and I'd slip in real quiet." His tongue darted into her ear, sending shivers through her. She had to close her eyes to try to fight off the desire that had begun to sizzle inside her. "I'd wake you with kisses every morning," he whispered, sliding his hand into her blouse and unclasping her bra. His thumb began to work magic on her nipple. "Would you like that, Monica?"

She took a shaky breath and tried to push his hand away. "I don't think that's a very good idea ..."

"No?" His thumb had aroused her nipple to a hardened bud. He cupped her breasts in his palms and began massaging them. "Well, then, I could come over to your office every day at lunch. Would that be better?"

Monica pictured Marc making love to her on the couch in her office while Terry and an assortment of clients waited in the reception room. The way Marc made her feel, she'd be lucky if she got any work done all afternoon. "Uh...no," she murmured. "I don't think so."

"Then we'll have to meet every night." He ran a hand into her panties and began caressing the pulsing ache at the junction of her legs. "You can come to my place sometimes, and sometimes I'll go to yours. How does that sound?"

Monica couldn't think. Her heart was pounding and his fingers were driving her mad with desire. She slid from a sitting position until she was stretched out on her side next to him on the floor. "I think that would be fine," she managed to say between kisses.

"Which?" he asked, coaxing her with drugging kisses while he took off her clothes. "My place or yours?"

"Doesn't matter," she whispered raggedly, digging her fingers into his back. "Anywhere you want is fine with me."

"What if I want you in the mornings sometimes?" he whispered, his fingers finding the exact spot that gave her the most incredible pleasure.

"We..." she inhaled sharply, then let her breath out on a ragged gasp of pleasure. "We could arrange something, I'm sure."

"Weekends at my place?" Marc suggested, rolling her onto her back and tracing his tongue down her abdomen. "You could come over Friday night and stay until Monday morning. That would give me three mornings with you."

She groaned audibly as his tongue flicked over her soft, pulsing center. "I...I don't know."

His tongue slid over the spot he knew gave her the most pleasure. "What can I do to convince you?" he whispered.

"Oh, Marc," she whispered, reaching for him. "I think you just have...."

Ten

Monica tapped her pen on her pristine desktop as she read over the latest proposal from real-estate developer Clay Firestone. When she finished reading it, she swiveled around in her chair to look out the window. The colorful autumn leaves were almost gone, and a leaden November sky loomed overhead, looking as if it might produce snow any moment.

On a whim, she picked up her phone, punched in Marc's number, then smiled when she heard his voice. "Hi," she said in the low sexy voice she reserved for him. "Getting any work done?"

"Not now I'm not," he said cheerfully. "What's up? You're coming over tonight, aren't you?"

"I'm coming," she said, smiling. In truth, she wouldn't miss it for the world. For the past two weekends, she'd gone to Marc's apartment directly from work on Friday afternoon, and she hadn't missed her Vermont cabin in the least.

Right now, her bag was packed and waiting in the car. After work, she'd drive into Hartford and park her car in the underground parking garage at Marc's Bushnell Plaza apartment, and she wouldn't get in it again until she drove back to Farmington on Monday morning.

"I'm preparing something special for dinner tonight," Marc said.

"You are?" She toyed with the phone wire, her eyes dreamy, a smile wreathing her face. "What is it?"

"A surprise, so don't even bother trying to worm it out of me."

"Then why'd you even mention it?"

"I just wanted to tease you."

"There are other ways you can tease me," she murmured in her huskiest voice.

"Nicky," Marc warned, using the nickname he'd given her, "don't. I'm at work, and I've got to keep my head on straight. All I need is you talking sexy to me and I'll go off the deep end."

"What would happen if you went off the deep end?" she asked, chuckling softly.

"I'd grab my suit-coat and run out of here all the way to Farmington. Terry would see this panting, slobbering streak run by and then I'd be in your office, pitching woo to you on top of your desk."

"Now that I'd like to see."

"Don't tempt me. Hey, did you call for a reason, or can't you wait for tonight?"

Monica's smile evaporated as her eyes ran over the Firestone proposal. "I need to talk to you," she said, frowning. "And I didn't want to wait until tonight."

Marc's playful mood changed immediately. "Got a problem?"

"No, not really, it's just—" She broke off, wondering what was happening to her. She'd found herself going to

Marc with lots of things lately, asking his advice or opinion, or just talking to him to get things clear in her own mind. She'd found he was an excellent listener. More and more, she was beginning to depend on him for a lot more than fathering her child.

"Clay Firestone dropped off a new development proposal with me," she said at last. "And this time he's gone too far."

"You mean the Fairmont Hotel deal?"

"How'd you know?" she asked, startled.

"Hey, Monica, I may be a criminal lawyer but I do read the paper. I also have lunch with plenty of city and state people. I know he bought the place and hired an architect to do some renderings. Last I heard, he's planning a parking garage under an office tower, with the top ten floors as luxury condos."

"That's about right," Monica said, "except he's added a shopping mall on the first two floors." She shook her head wearily. "Hartford can't support another major shopping plaza, and we sure as heck don't need more office space. We're going to end up like Houston and Dallas—overdeveloped without the business to fill the spaces."

"So what are you talking to me for? Tell him what you think."

"I plan to, but I wanted to run an idea by you."

"Shoot."

"I'd like to try to talk him into preserving the Fairmont. With the old Hartford Hotel leveled, the Fairmont is the last of the old beauties. What Hartford needs desperately is housing. I think he should renovate the hotel and make it into apartments or condos. It's a fantastic location, and there's enough room to build a small parking garage on one site. I think it would be perfect."

"He wouldn't make as much money though," Marc said.

"Yeah, I know," Monica responded glumly. "And money's the name of the development game, isn't it?"

"Usually," Marc said. "But if I were you, I'd suggest it. It sure can't hurt."

"Thanks, Marc." She hesitated. "You know, you're the most supportive man I've ever known."

"You run that idea by Firestone and we'll take a walk by the Fairmont this weekend, okay?"

"Okay, and Marc? Thanks."

"Don't mention it. See you around six."

Monica hung up, then dialed Clay Firestone's office. Like Marc said, it wouldn't hurt to try....

"Clay Firestone is an imbecile," Monica said angrily, throwing down her coat and striding briskly across Marc's plush wall-to-wall carpeting toward his bedroom. As she walked, she unbuttoned and unzipped, so that by the time she was in the bedroom, she was out of her suit and blouse and rummaging in her bag for the outfit she would wear tonight. "He's got the vision of a bat," she said, slamming the suitcase shut and heading for the bathroom.

Marc lounged against the doorjamb, watching her as she turned on the shower and crammed her hair into a shower cap. "Where's my kiss?" he asked, grinning at her agitated motions that indicated how angry she was.

"Oh!" She went to him and kissed him quickly, then put her arms around him for another. "See what a jerk Clay Firestone is?" she murmured when the kiss ended. "He made me so angry I forgot how great it is to kiss you."

"Take your shower," Marc said, grinning. "I'll have a drink ready for you when you get out."

In the shower, Monica soaped herself thoughtfully. In just a month, she and Marc had become so comfortable with each other that she sometimes felt like they were married. At least this would be her dream version of marriage, if she didn't know from observation what marriage was really like.

But Marc was happy because he had a willing bed partner along with his bachelor freedom. He had the benefits of marriage with none of the responsibilities. Things would change if they were truly married. Marriage vows were like the kiss of death—the moment they were uttered, love and affection were doomed. After that, a couple who might have lived together blissfully for years usually changed overnight into shrill, bickering contestants in a domestic war.

Monica dressed, then wandered toward the kitchen. It was too bad she had no illusions about marriage, or she'd be tempted to try it with Marc. She liked his apartment with its sweeping view of the state capital and Bushnell Park. It was amazing how quickly she'd learned to feel at home here—she normally found modern furniture too cold. But Marc's furniture was well designed, and accented with a few antique pieces, which had surprised and delighted her.

In the kitchen, Marc was cutting vegetables and flipping them into a wok. Her drink sat on the counter next to his.

"Stir-fry?" she asked, sipping her drink gratefully and helping herself to a piece of raw cauliflower.

"Yeah," Marc said. "I'm doing Chinese food."

"Well, I hope it's better than your pot roast last weekend," Monica said lightly.

Marc lunged for her, and she complied by not trying to get away. "The pot roast was edible," he said between kisses.

She put her arms around his neck and laughed softly. "Uh-uh. It was horrible."

"Nicky," Marc said warningly, "take that back, or I'll make you cook."

"Oh, well, in that case I think your cooking is great. It's terrific. Every chef in Connecticut should tremble in his *toque blanche*."

"Why do I get the impression you're insincere?" Marc wondered out loud, letting her go and returning to his cooking. "Let's get off the subject of food. What's wrong with Clay Firestone?"

"Nothing that a lobotomy wouldn't cure," Monica said darkly.

Marc began to chuckle. "I take it he didn't appreciate your idea about the Fairmont."

"Appreciate it?" Monica laughed humorlessly. "He almost had apoplexy. He said he wasn't a philanthropist, he was a businessman. He said my father must be rolling in his grave right now." Monica sighed heavily. "Marc, something's happening to me."

Marc looked up. "Oh?" he asked casually. "What?"

She shrugged irritably. "I don't know. I can't put a finger on it. It's just I feel so restless. I want...I want..." She stared into space, her face mirroring her frustration and puzzlement. "I don't know what I want," she finished lamely. "All I know is I don't like my life the way it is right now."

Marc frowned, concentrating on dicing celery. "Maybe you need more space," he said quietly. "Maybe spending every night with me and every weekend at my place is beginning to get to you."

"No!" she said automatically, without even thinking, "that's not it at all. In fact, that's the only part of my life I *do* enjoy. It's work that's bothering me. It's divorces and real-estate development. Sitting in my office, I sometimes get the feeling that everyone in the world is either fighting or cutting a big deal that's going to make them millionaires."

"Why'd you become a lawyer, Nicky?"

"To please my father," she said, then met Marc's eyes. "But I'm a good lawyer, Marc."

"A good one, but not a happy one."

She nodded glumly. "Dad was the best divorce lawyer in the state," she said. "And real estate—he always told me real estate was where the money was." She sighed heavily. "He was right, of course. He was always right." She stared out the window toward the gold dome of the state capital, illuminated against the night sky. "No, he wasn't," she said slowly. "There were lots of things he wasn't right about."

"Seems to me it's time you started living your own life, Nicky, rather than the one your father envisioned for you."

"But I've begun to, Marc. That's what having the baby is all about."

Marc frowned. "I don't get the connection between your finally having a baby and your father. Didn't he want you to have children?"

Monica stiffened. She'd gotten so comfortable with Marc that she'd begun to open up. If she wasn't careful, she might tell him more than she wanted to. "He wanted me to become a lawyer first and foremost, Marc. When I was dating Andy Emerson, Dad interfered. He sent me to Europe the summer between my sophomore and junior years at college. Unfortunately, Andy misunderstood about that summer and we broke up for good. If I'd married Andy, I would have started a family soon."

"Didn't you have anything to say for yourself? I mean, it was your life, Nicky, not your dad's."

Monica turned her back and sipped her drink, playing for time. These were the same questions she'd spent years asking herself. If she hadn't answered them adequately for herself, how could she answer them for Marc?

"Nicky?" Marc came up behind her and put a hand on her arm. "You okay?"

She smiled quickly. "I'm fine."

He looked at her thoughtfully, and slowly shook his head. "No you're not. You're hiding something. I haven't spent the last four weeks with you without learning at least that much about you."

"Marc, I don't want to talk about it, okay? Sure, I can look back now and say I was stupid to let Dad run my life. It was the biggest mistake of my life, and believe me, I'm still paying for it. But I did let him. I loved him, Marc. He was this great shining knight in my eyes, and I would have walked over hot coals for him."

She broke off and turned away, but the words kept coming. "All I ever wanted was for him to love me," she said quietly, "but he never once told me he did. I spent my entire life trying to get him to say it. Once would have been enough. I did everything I could think of—I studied, I worked harder than anyone else I knew, I even gave up my—" She broke off in confusion. "I even gave up Andy and became a lawyer to please him, and it still wasn't enough." She closed her eyes and rubbed the icy cold glass against her forehead, letting the cold burn out the beginnings of her headache.

Marc came up behind her and slid his arms around her waist, drawing her back against his chest and holding her as she continued to talk. "It wasn't until I graduated from law school that I realized I'd never get what I wanted. My father was the coldest man on earth. I don't think he knew the meaning of the word love, much less how to give it."

"I hope you realize it was your dad's fault, not yours, that he wasn't able to express his love for you."

"Express his love!" Monica broke from Marc's arms and turned to confront him, her eyes blazing. "*Express* it? The man didn't have any to give in the first place, Marc. Don't go defending him. He didn't love me, he didn't love my mother, he wouldn't have loved his grandchild. Don't talk to me about him. You don't know anything about him, nothing at all."

"I know he was proud of you. One of the first things I remember people talking about was how proud he was of you. I remember expecting you to be an amazon or something, dedicated only to your work, because all Jason Bliss ever talked about was his daughter, the lady lawyer. He was so damned proud of you, Monica, that his eyes shone. He didn't stand around the Hartford Club talking about *his* deals, he stood around talking about *yours*. Maybe he never told you he loved you, but he *showed* that love all over town."

Confounded, Monica stared at Marc. In all the time she'd worked as a lawyer, no one had ever told her anything like this. "I don't believe you," she said, feeling numb.

"Okay," Marc said, turning angrily on his heel, "don't."

She stared at his rigid back, seeing the hurt radiate from him. "Marc," she said, going to him and placing a hand on his arm. "I'm sorry."

He looked at her, shaking his head. "You can't believe anyone could ever love you, can you?"

"Not my father," she said, her eyes filled with sorrow. "He did something—it doesn't matter what—but it was so cruel, Marc, so unfeeling, that he *couldn't* have loved me."

"Maybe he did whatever he did *because* he loved you. Maybe to him he was doing what he thought was best for you. People don't always love us the way we want to be loved, you know, Nicky. Sometimes people love us the only way they know how."

She felt tears begin to fill her eyes and she didn't know what to do. Tears were private affairs. You didn't share them with others. She stood blinking, feeling her throat close up so that she couldn't even speak, then Marc groaned softly and took her in his arms and she collapsed against him, crying into his shirt, clutching at him, sobbing like a child.

"I'm sorry," she whispered brokenly. "I know men hate women who cry."

"This man doesn't," Marc said, stroking her hair gently. "You sure make a hell of a lot of assumptions, Nicky."

She leaned back into his arms. "You mean you don't mind my crying? Look! I've ruined your shirt. It's all wet, and my face probably looks terrible—all running mascara and smeared lipstick. And my eyes get red when I cry, and my nose looks like some old drunk's, and—"

"Hush, will you?" he asked, drawing her into his arms again and cradling her against him. "If you think I can't put up with your smeared mascara you can't think very much of me. How you look isn't what matters, Monica. Who you are and what you feel are all that are important to me."

She stared unseeingly, vividly aware of his warm chest and strong arms, of the even rise and fall of his breathing, of feeling warm and protected and safe. Slowly, she began to rub her cheek against his chest. "You feel so good," she whispered, closing her eyes and reveling in the feelings that pervaded her. "I feel so safe with you."

"Good," he murmured, dropping kisses on her hair. "That's the way it should be between us." He hugged her tighter. "That's the way I want it always to be, Nicky."

She smiled. "I like it how you call me Nicky."

"Yeah?"

She nodded, smiling wider. "I've never liked my name very much."

"I like it," Marc said, grinning down at her. "But then I like everything about you, so I guess I'm prejudiced."

She stared into his eyes, knowing something important had just been said without being said at all. She had the strongest urge to say something too, something equally as nice about Marc, but something held her back. She wasn't a giving person, she realized. She was too used to holding back. When she had a baby, she'd need to learn how to share feelings, become intimate. She didn't want to do to her own child what her father and mother had done to her.

"I like you, too," she said suddenly, feeling awkward, like a child trying out her first pair of roller skates. "I like you a lot."

"Hold that thought," he said, turning back to his cooking. "If you can make it through my Chinese food without changing your mind, we just might have a chance together."

Monica's smile faltered, then slowly faded. "Don't, Marc. Don't assume that just because we've been happy this past month that anything further is going to happen. It's not. I want a child, not a husband."

A muscle worked in Marc's jaw, but he shrugged in apparent unconcern. "So who's wanting anything more?" he asked, raising a wry brow over eyes that gleamed with amusement. "Things are just fine the way they are now," he said, tossing a crouton in the air and catching it in his mouth. "Don't *you* go making assumptions, Nicky, okay? Let's just enjoy ourselves the way we are."

She should have been relieved, but instead she was disappointed, which in turn made her angry. Dammit, things were fine just the way they were. Marc was right. She just wished *he* wished things were different, that's all.

After supper, they bundled up and walked to the Fairmont Hotel in downtown Hartford. The ten-story brick building with broken window panes and chipped marble trim sat neglected, its double doors boarded up and the red-striped awning over the front entrance in tatters. In the glare of the streetlights, it seemed even more shabby and unkempt than during the day.

At the sight of the old hotel, Monica felt conflicting emotions rise up in her. Since her abortive attempt to convince Clay Firestone to renovate the Fairmont instead of razing it, she was having second thoughts about her ability to make an impact on the preservation of old buildings. All her initial excitement about a change in her career had drained away in the face of Clay Firestone's derision. Now she stood irresolute, wondering if she were just a dreamer.

"It looks sad," Monica said, staring at the seedy building. "It reminds me of an old actress, once beautiful but now ugly and forgotten. I remember watching a movie once about Lily Langtry. In the end she grew old and lost her beauty and no one remembered her, and I remember thinking how sad it was, to grow old and lose everything you ever had..." She shivered, and Marc put his arm around her.

"Buildings aren't people, Monica."

"No, but this building is like that—once it was the most beautiful building in Hartford, but now we've built new glass and granite towers and no one wants a dumpy old brick building with marble trim." She felt something cold go through her. "I don't like the world we're living in, Marc," she said suddenly. "I don't like the way we seem to think that newer and bigger is always better. We have this stupid love affair with the new, and I'm afraid we're going to lose touch with what we've been. In Europe, they venerate the past, but here..." She paused, too troubled to go on.

"Here, what?" Marc asked, prodding her to think through her thoughts.

"Here, we knock it down before we even think of preserving it. It's as if the past doesn't matter, that we only have eyes for the future. But what does that really mean, Marc? It means that what we have now isn't even worthwhile, because in the end, it won't matter either. Someday, our children will look around and see only bulldozers and pavement, and if they want to learn about their past, they'll have to look for it in history books and museums."

Marc shrugged. "If the past and if old buildings matter so much, the only way they're going to be saved is if people care enough to try to save them. You can stand here and wring your hands, but unfortunately it won't do a hell of a lot of good."

Listening to him, Monica felt the sting of her conscience, but for some reason, she couldn't share her doubts with Marc about a possible change in her career. She turned on her heel and stalked off. "Thanks," she said over her shoulder. "And earlier today I think I said you were the most supportive man I knew."

"You don't like what's happening in this world, Monica?" Marc said, catching up with her. "Then stop talking about it and do something."

She came to a thumping halt, then turned and met his gaze. He looked unfeeling, uncaring, and cold. "I can't change the world, Marc," she said coolly.

"No, but you can begin to work at changing part of it. If that damn hotel matters so much to you," he said, stabbing his finger at it, "then stop talking and start acting."

"I *did* act!" she shouted. "I talked with Clay Firestone and he laughed in my face."

"Fine. If that's the only action you can take, so be it. Just don't stand here and moan about the world going to hell and how helpless you are to do anything about it."

"Dammit, what do you want me to do? Shoot Clay Firestone? What more can I do. Grovel? Plead? Wear sackcloth and ashes and keep a vigil outside the damned place?"

"If it would work, sackcloth and ashes might not be a bad idea."

"Oh, Marc," she said disgustedly. "Be serious."

"No, Monica, you be serious. Dammit, you're a fine lawyer, and yet you act as if you haven't any power. You're right, maybe you can't do anything further for the Fairmont, but if you feel so strongly about preserving our past, then start doing *something* about it. There's a fine organization here in Hartford called The Rehab that works for historic preservation. Volunteer your time with them. Do their legal work for free. Get on their board. Attend their meetings. Start going to zoning board meetings. Put your money where your mouth is." Marc's face grew more and more angry, his words more agitated. "Dammit, Monica, you act as if you're a puppet, being led around on a string that someone out of sight is manipulating. When are you going to learn that it's *your* life, not your father's? When the hell is it going to hit you that you can do what you *want* to do, not what's *expected* of you?"

She stared at him, then said quietly, "This isn't about the Fairmont at all, is it? It's about why I won't marry you."

"*You* won't marry *me*?" Marc laughed out loud. "Listen to the woman! Has it ever occurred to you that I wouldn't want to marry a woman who has ice water in her veins?"

Monica felt as if she'd been struck. Two vivid spots of color surged into her cheeks. Turning on her heel, she began walking as fast as she could toward Marc's apartment.

Marc caught up with her. "I'm sorry," he said, his face tormented, his eyes wretched. "I didn't mean that."

She stopped walking. "I believe we always say what we really mean, especially when we're angry."

"No, Monica, sometimes we say what we know will hurt the other person," he said. "I wanted to hurt you because you hit a nerve. You're right, this argument *is* about your not wanting to marry me." He thrust his hand through his hair distractedly. "But dammit, Monica, just when I think you're beginning to really care for me, just when it seems we're beginning to get really close, you tell me not to get any ideas. Why shouldn't I get some ideas? You make love with me practically every night trying to get pregnant with my child. Is it too much to assume you might fall in love with me? Am I asking too much to want to discuss the possibility of marriage?"

She backed away from him, frightened as much by her own reaction to what he was saying as by the vehemence in his voice or the passion in his face. If he continued chipping away at her, she'd stop fighting him, and she couldn't stop fighting. It wasn't safe. Maybe someday, years from now, she'd be able to stop fighting him, but not yet. Not tonight, not tomorrow, not even next month.

"Don't force me, Marc," she said, coming to a stop with her back against a building. "Please, don't force me."

"Oh, Nicky," he said, taking her in his arms and crushing her against his chest, "I won't force you. I swear I won't, honey. Just don't shut me out. Promise me you'll some day tell me what you're frightened of."

She closed her eyes and clung to him, her throat closed up so that she could barely speak. "Okay," she said, but inside, she crossed her fingers and whispered, "Some day, perhaps..."

Eleven

A week later, Monica's office phone rang. Without looking up from her work, she stabbed the button and picked it up. "Monica Bliss."

A well-modulated voice greeted her, "Monica, this is Eleanor English, Marc's mother."

Monica stared, dumbfounded, then managed to find her voice. "Why, Mrs. English, how nice to hear from you."

"Marc tells me he's been seeing a lot of you," Mrs. English said with a smile in her voice. "Unfortunately, if I waited for him to bring you home and introduce you, I'd be in one of those dastardly nursing homes somewhere, knitting and picking lint off my lap robe. I'd very much like you to come to tea with me this afternoon. I know you must be terribly busy, but I'd very much like to meet you and have a chance to chat."

"Why, Mrs. English..." Monica said, feeling pleased and nervous at the same time, "that would be lovely. Of course I'll come. I'd be delighted."

"Good, I'll expect you about four, then. You know where we live?"

"Yes, ma'am."

"I'm so happy you'll come, Monica," Mrs. English said, sounding as excited as a young girl. "See you at four."

"Goodbye." Monica hung up and stared in bemusement at the phone. An invitation to tea with Eleanor English. She remembered seeing her at social events—dances at the golf club, parties at the Wadsworth Atheneum, concerts at the Bushnell. She'd always been impeccably dressed and coiffed, always smiling and gracious, tall, trim, and elegant, yet filled with warmth—Monica's ideal of the perfect lady.

Monica looked down at herself, feeling a strange thrill at finally meeting a woman she'd only recognized on sight. She would definitely have to go home and change into something more suitable than her navy wool business suit.

Monica smoothed a nervous hand over her coat, then walked up the winding brick sidewalk toward the imposing entrance to the English home on Prospect Street. She grasped the brass knocker on the black enameled door and struck it forcefully, then stood looking at the white-painted brick upon which ivy climbed in carefully sculpted luxury.

The door was opened by an elderly white-haired woman in a black dress. "Ms. Bliss? I'm Mrs. Hankins. Mrs. English is expecting you."

Monica gave the housekeeper her coat, then glanced around surreptitiously at the wide entrance hall. A gold-framed mirror hung on the wall over a mahogany sideboard on which stood an arrangement of mums and eucalyptus. Old but beautifully cared for Oriental rugs were scattered on the highly waxed floor. A gracious staircase ascended to the second floor, its risers covered in a royal blue carpet.

She was ushered into a high-ceilinged room where a fire roared in a marble fireplace. The walls were covered in a bright floral print that matched the chintz-covered couch and wing chairs. A slender, elegantly dressed woman with silver hair sat on one end of the couch. In front of her the tea service was set on the coffee table. The woman stood up, extending her slim, wrinkled hand to Monica and smiling graciously.

"Monica, I'm so happy to meet you."

"I'm pleased to meet you, Mrs. English."

"Please sit here, dear," Mrs. English said, indicating a seat next to her on the couch. Smiling, she settled down next to Monica, her bright blue eyes sparkling with open curiosity. "Well!" she said, "Marc was right. You're perfectly beautiful."

Monica felt unexpected color blossom in her pale cheeks. "You're very kind to invite me for tea, Mrs. English," she said, looking around at the graciously inviting room. "Your home is lovely."

"Thank you, my dear," the older woman said, pouring tea. "Lemon?"

"Please."

"*Now* then," Eleanor English said, handing Monica her tea and picking up her own cup, "Marc tells me you're a lawyer, specializing in divorce and real-estate law. Do you like your work?"

Monica was about to give a polite social answer when something told her not to. Eleanor English looked genuinely interested and Monica thought she would appreciate honesty more than social manners. "Actually, I love working, but I'm not too happy with what I do lately."

"Mmm," Eleanor said, nodding. "Marc intimated something of the sort. He mentioned how upset you are at the Fairmont's imminent demise."

"Upset is putting it mildly," Monica said, smiling. "I even went so far as to try to talk Clay Firestone out of it. Unfortunately, that didn't work."

"The Fairmont has always been a rather special place for me, too. Mr. English and I had our wedding reception there."

"Did you? It must have been beautiful."

"It was. It got a wonderful write-up in the papers. But..." The older woman shrugged. "It looks as if another magnificent part of our past will be leveled. We at the Rehab have tried to save it, but men like Clay Firestone have much more money than we, so quite often all we can do is protest and try to rouse public opinion."

"The Rehab?"

"I'm on the board of the Hartford Neighborhood Rehabilitation Center. We've had some marvelous success—the Congress Street and Frog Hollow areas most notably—but for the most part, we haven't been able to fight the really big downtown developers. It broke my heart when that Wilson man, or whatever his name is, leveled the State Street buildings and put up that mess."

"I had no idea you were on the Rehab board," Monica said slowly. "That explains why Marc was so angry with me last week. He told me to stop whining and get involved in a group that's working on preserving old buildings. He never once mentioned you, though." Monica looked up from her tea. "Oh, now I see why I'm here," she said.

"No," Eleanor said, shaking her head. "We happen to share an interest, which I thought I'd capitalize on, but I didn't invite you here to convince you to work at The Rehab. I invited you here so I could meet the woman I hope will marry my son."

"Oh." Monica had to look away from the older woman's knowing blue eyes. "I see . . ."

"I'm sorry. I've upset you. How thoughtless of me."

"No I . . . I . . . Not at all!" Confused, Monica looked at Marc's mother, not knowing what to say. How did one explain to a woman that her son was being used in a kind of medical experiment? "I . . . I think the world of Marc. I care for him very much," she said, dropping her gaze to her tea. "It's just that I . . . well, I don't really have any plans to marry."

It was Eleanor's turn to look confused. "I see. Well!" She sat up straight, in obvious discomfort. "You young people puzzle me. When Mr. English and I were young, we thought it was natural to get married." She frowned and set down the fragile china cup. "I've so wanted Marc to marry," she said, sounding suddenly old and tired. "I thought this time he'd finally found the woman he wanted. He's so *picky*, you see. Ten years ago he came close to being engaged, but in the end it didn't work out, then a couple of years ago, he told me there was only one woman for him, but she wouldn't have him. He wouldn't say much beyond that, and of course I didn't pry. That's why I was so happy when he told me he was seeing you. I thought at last he'd gotten over this other woman and might settle down."

Monica tilted her head inquiringly. "Did he say who this other woman was?"

"No, he just said she was the only woman for him, but he'd made a huge mistake with her and she'd turned him away." Eleanor sighed, then poured herself another cup. "More tea, dear?"

"No, thank you," Monica said, her thoughts in chaos. Could she possibly be the other woman that Marc had wanted for the past two years? But he'd made it so clear that he hadn't really been interested in anything beyond sleeping with her. . . .

"I hope you'll join Marc and my husband and me for Thanksgiving dinner, Monica. It's an English family tradition. We're not a *big* family—Marc's our only child—but we're a warm and loving one." She smiled sadly. "I've so wanted grandchildren...."

Eleanor's words went through Monica like a lance. Suddenly she felt weak. How was she going to handle this extraordinary mess? When Marc was just a man, disembodied from his family, it hadn't seemed so bad to ask him to father her child, but *now*.... Monica lifted her gaze to the older woman and saw the veiled sadness in her eyes, saw the deep wrinkles in her face, the hands that seemed so utterly fragile, and suddenly Monica realized that if she bore Marc's child, she would also be bearing Eleanor English's grandchild. Perhaps her only grandchild.

"You *will* come for Thanksgiving dinner, won't you, dear?" Eleanor said, breaking into Monica's thoughts.

"Why, yes," Monica said, feeling a strange combination of apprehension and compassion come over her. "Yes, I'd love to."

The very idea of spending Thanksgiving dinner with the Englishes made Monica uneasy. She stood in her bedroom that morning, staring at her clothes in her walk-in closet, wondering what to wear.

Marc had no such worries. If things were left up to him, they wouldn't join his parents at all. For some reason, when she'd told him that his mother had invited her to tea, and there had extended an invitation to share the family Thanksgiving, he'd begun to grumble and take on as if that were the last thing he wanted. His idea of Thanksgiving dinner was probably staying in bed and making love all day. She'd only escaped by climbing quietly out of bed before he'd woken up.

"Nicky?" Marc's sleepy morning voice broke into her reverie.

"I'm here, Marc," she called from the depths of the closet. "Trying to decide what to wear."

"Don't decide too quickly," he yelled, running toward the bathroom. "I'll be right out."

Despite herself, Monica had to smile. After almost six weeks with Marc, he still made her feel entirely desirable. He seemed never to tire of her, never to be bored with her company. He'd done more for her ego in six weeks than any other man in her life. She heard the shower go on, heard Marc's roar of protest at the icy water, and began to chuckle.

How she loved this morning routine they'd developed. Ever thoughtful, Marc would put off making love to her until he'd showered and shaved and brushed his teeth. She'd tried to tell him that it didn't matter, but he wouldn't listen. Instead, he always made a beeline for the shower, not even waiting for the water to heat properly, then shaved quickly and brushed his teeth. After he was dry he would run back to bed and cover her with kisses, kisses that still burned into her soul.

"What are you smiling about, Nicky?" Marc murmured, coming up behind her and putting his arms around her. He nuzzled the side of her neck and pulled her back against his naked chest. "Do I make you happy, honey?"

She closed her eyes and felt happiness soar inside her. "Oh, yes, Marc," she said huskily. "You make me very happy."

He began to unbutton her silk pajama top. "You make me happy, too," he murmured, sliding a hand into her top to cup her breast. "In bed and out, day and night. I lo—" He coughed suddenly, but then he turned her around in his arms, smothering her with kisses. "I lust after you," he said in a Count Dracula voice. "I *love* your neck, your breasts, your pretty little belly."

"Marc!" she said, laughing and trying to push him away as his tongue tickled her abdomen. "Stop!"

"Never!" he said, picking her up and carrying her toward the bed. "You're my woman." He dropped her onto the bed and stood beating his chest. "Me, He-Man. You, my woman. We mate."

"You big fool," she said softly, her eyes filled with warmth. She shook her head at the disappointed look on his face. Reaching up, she took his hand. "Come 'ere, He-Man," she murmured huskily, "your woman wants you."

"What does she want?" he asked, settling his body over hers, covering her with steamy kisses. "Hmm?" he murmured, sliding his tongue over and around her nipple, rousing it to pebble hardness. He slid his hand between her legs. "This?" He rubbed his fingers back and forth against her sensitive skin. "Or this?" He covered her with his body, pressing his arousal against her. "Is this what she wants?"

Breathlessly, Monica wrapped her arms around him and raised her hips, opening her legs to him. "Yes," she whispered. "This."

He entered her gently, then eased into her, exhaling with pleasure as he sank deeper and deeper. "You feel so good," he crooned in her ear. "So silky, so smooth. What do I feel like to you?"

She found it difficult to think, much less talk coherently, but she tried. "You feel strong," she said, beginning to breathe erratically as her senses roused toward a climax. "Strong and warm," she whispered. "So good, Marc. You're so perfect inside me."

"Tell me how you feel," he whispered, his breathing tormented as he quickened his rhythm and thrust into her more deeply.

"I..." She closed her eyes in rapture, clinging to him, her head thrown back, her legs locked around his waist. "I..." He thrust deeper, frenzied, driving her further and further toward the cliff, until her fingernails dug into his broad back and she felt herself slipping into ecstasy. "Oh, Marc," she breathed. "Don't stop, you feel so wonderful."

"Tell me how you feel," he demanded, thrusting harder and deeper, yet keeping her just on the brink.

"I..." She felt the wave begin, felt it breaking over her in glorious splendor, felt her body being torn apart. "I love you!" she cried as she fell into the swirling center. "*I love you.*"

"I love you, too," Marc said later, lying on his side, one arm thrown over her, looking into her eyes.

She couldn't speak, couldn't move, could only lie on her back and look into his eyes, barely believing the miracle that had occurred in her life. She felt tears well up in her eyes and didn't try to blink them away or hide them. She let them trail softly down her face, and exhaled a happy, tremulous breath when Marc began to kiss them away.

"I love you," she whispered brokenly, smiling and laughing and crying all at once. "I love you so much. Oh, Marc," she whispered, "Marc, tell me again."

"I love you," he said, kissing her tears, her eyelids, her nose, her lips. "I adore you," he whispered, kissing her earlobe, her neck, the hollow of her throat. "I love you, Monica Marie Bliss, in every wonderful way it's possible for a man to love a woman."

She smiled tremulously, still crying, so incredibly happy she couldn't believe her good fortune. "Say it again."

He kissed her deeply, his tongue entering her mouth and circling hers. "I love you," he said at last. "Marry me."

She stared up at him, and suddenly landed on earth. "Marry you?"

"Yes, you know—you wear a white dress and I wear my tux, and we say these vows, and there's flowers and candles on the altar, and then we live together happily ever after, having little babies and buying a house in the country, and a station wagon. You know, Nicky—marriage."

She felt a knot form in her throat, felt her heart begin to pound painfully. Suddenly, her happiness had vanished. She looked into his eyes and could see only Andy's eyes, hear Andy's words, crashing at her, shouted, hurt, angry. He hadn't been able to understand how she'd been able to give up their child without his even knowing it had existed. He'd backed away from her, looking at her as if she were unlovable and unloved. "How could you do it, Monica?" he kept asking, over and over. "How *could* you?"

"Monica?" Marc's concerned voice broke into the nightmarish memory. "Monica, are you all right?"

She nodded, trembling. She was nauseated, sickened by the memory. "I feel a little sick," she said, forcing herself to sit up. Her head swirled, her temples pounded, her palms grew sweaty. "I'll be all right," she said, swallowing, trying to force her stomach to settle itself. "I'm just a little taken aback by your proposal, I guess," she joked. "I think I need a little time to think it over."

"Here, let me get you a cool towel for your forehead," Marc said, striding toward the bathroom. "You look really pale," he said when he returned. "Are you sure you're all right?"

"I'm fine," she assured him, taking the wet towel gratefully and wiping her face. "That'll teach you to ask me to marry you," she said, forcing a laugh.

Marc sat down on the edge of the bed, his face serious. "Maybe we shouldn't go to my parents'. I'll call and tell them you're not feeling well."

"Of course we'll go," she said. "I'll be fine in a minute or two. You just took me by surprise." She looked up at him curiously. "How come you don't want to go to your parents' today?"

He shrugged, looking too innocent. "I want to go. I'm just worried about you, that's all."

She shook her head, her eyes narrowed. "Uh-uh. I keep getting the feeling you didn't like it that your mother invited me to tea and issued the invitation for today." She tilted her head inquiringly. "Don't you want your parents to meet me?"

"Of course I want them to meet you, Nicky," Marc said, taking her hand. "I guess I'm just being selfish. If I can keep you to myself a little longer, I want to, but I guess I'll just have to risk it."

"Risk it?" she asked, laughing in puzzlement.

He shrugged, looking like a kid. "Maybe you'll find out you don't like my family. Maybe an old skeleton will fall out of the closet at you, or something."

"Oh, sure," she said, deadpan. "A skeleton in the English family closet? Not likely. Anyway, I like your mother already. She's such a lady. And I'm sure I'll like your dad, as well."

Marc frowned. "They'll probably bug us about getting married, Nicky. They're getting older, you know, and they want me to marry and have kids. You better be prepared."

"As a matter of fact, your mother already broached the subject," Monica said.

"What did you say?"

Monica looked away. She felt strangely queasy again. All this talk about marriage was getting to her. "I said I wasn't ready to settle down."

"I see." Marc nodded grimly. "I'll wait, then," he said. "As long as it takes, I'll wait." He stood up and looked down at her, clearly troubled but determined to allow her the time she needed. "I need another shower. Join me?"

She shook her head, forcing another smile. "No, you go on. I'll take one later."

He nodded, then bent and kissed her gently on the forehead. "I love you, Nicky. That's enough for now."

She watched him walk into the bathroom and shut the door, then she closed her eyes and tried to stop the pain that felt like a sword in her heart. He loved her because he didn't really know her. If he ever found out what she was really like, what she'd done all those years ago, he would never be able to honestly say those words to her again.

Suppressing a moan of pain, Monica sat up and held her head. She felt utterly lousy. What a great way to feel on the day the man she loved had asked her to marry him.

Twelve

Snowflakes began to drift from the slate gray sky while Marc and Monica drove to his parents' house.

"It's snowing, Nicky," Marc said, looking at her with a huge smile and taking her hand. "I've always loved the first snow of the season."

She squeezed his hand, her eyes filled with love. "You're a big guy, Marc English, but inside you're still a little kid."

"Sure," he said, grinning. "We've all got some child left in us. That's the fun part, the part that laughs and plays jokes and teases." He narrowed his eyes and looked at her speculatively. "When I first met you, I didn't think you had any child in you at all. You were all adult, always thinking about work. Thank God I came into your life."

"You're full of baloney," she said, laughing.

Except, of course, he wasn't. He was right—she had been repressed, dull and businesslike. She hadn't laughed much, hadn't even cried, but being with Marc had taught her to live life to the fullest. Now she laughed a lot, cried at times, she yelled and shouted, and if Marc wasn't careful, someday she just might throw a downright tantrum.

Yet something told her that wouldn't frighten him. He'd probably throw one right back at her. The wonderful thing about Marc was that he was *whole*. He was real and genuine, and in touch with every part of himself. Unlike Monica, he hadn't cut off his feelings, hadn't disconnected from humanity.

But then again, Marc didn't have anything to hide. There couldn't possibly be anything that would prevent him from reaching out to others for fear of discovery.

"Hey," Marc said, "you're slipping away, Nicky."

"What do you mean?"

"You get this way sometimes," he explained, turning into Prospect Street. "You get lost in your thoughts and you go all quiet on me. Which wouldn't be bad, except you get that sad look in your eyes, as if there's this terrible sorrow that you can't exorcise." He pulled the car up in front of his parents' home and cut the engine, then put his arm over the back of her seat and began toying with a strand of her hair. "That's when I begin to feel helpless. I begin to feel there's nothing I can do to get you to open up to me, to share with me. I don't want a fair-weather relationship with you, I want it all—the good and the bad. I want a *life* with you, not a glossy picture in a magazine, where everything looks great on the surface but is really cold and nothing more than appearance."

She closed her eyes and rested her head against the seat, troubled yet hopeful. She rolled her head to the side and smiled at him. "You want a lot," she said quietly.

He nodded. "Everything."

"Sometimes we can't have everything."

"Sometimes we can."

"Your glass is always half-full, isn't it, Marc?" she asked, smiling softly. "You're eternally optimistic."

"Yes, I guess that's true. I think life is essentially wonderful, that people are essentially good. But then I've been raised by two wonderful, loving people who fostered that belief. I didn't have to put up with a home life like you had, so maybe it's easier for me to see the glass half-full, as you put it, rather than half-empty."

She reached out and touched his face, her eyes filled with love. "I've never been happier in my life than I have these past six weeks, Marc. I feel warmer, more real. I . . . I *feel*. I'm not just existing anymore. I'm living."

Marc took her hand and pressed a kiss into her palm. "I love you, Nicky. I think I could make your life like this forever, not just for six weeks. I believe we all have the ability to make our lives what we want them to be. We don't have to just live from day to day in sheer drudgery. I think we have to allow ourselves to dream, to believe in love and joy and miracles. If I've made you happy these six weeks, I'll make you ten times happier for the rest of our lives. You already know you want my child, you've admitted you love me. Take the last step, Nicky. Allow yourself to have the life you dreamed about but never thought you could have. Marry me."

"Oh, Marc." She went into his arms, pressing her eyes shut in ecstasy, glorying in the warmth of his embrace, the way his strong arms held her, making her feel cherished and protected.

"Will you?" he asked, pressing kisses on her eyelids, her nose, her ear.

"No," she said, then relented almost immediately. "Maybe."

"Yes," he urged, his breath urgent in her ear. "Say yes, Nicky. Say yes."

She pushed away, toying with a button on his shirt, her eyes troubled. "We need to talk a lot more, Marc," she said quietly. "There's so much you don't know about me."

"I know, honey," he said, holding her close. "There are things you don't know about me, too, but we can deal with those things."

Something in his voice bothered her. She sat back and looked into his face, but whatever was there disappeared. Brightening, he grinned at her, pulling her into his arms and smothering her with kisses.

"Marc!" she protested laughingly. "My makeup!"

"The hell with your makeup," he growled. "I like you without makeup. I like your lips all swollen from my kisses, and your cheeks red from my beard, and your eyes glowing from my lovemaking."

"Would your parents?" she asked dryly.

He made a fist and tapped her under her chin. "Always worried about what people think, huh, Monica Marie?"

She shrugged and smoothed a hand over her black wool dress. "I don't think it hurts to make a good impression, Marc," she said, smiling. "I doubt your parents would appreciate your bringing home a woman who looked like you'd just dragged her into the nearest haystack and had your way with her."

Marc sighed. "Okay, I'll behave. Just don't be surprised if I play footsie with you under the table at dinner."

"You wouldn't."

"Wouldn't I?" he asked gravely. "Just wait and see."

He was out of the car then, hurrying around the side to open her door, then holding out his hand to snare a snowflake. Laughing, they raced up the winding sidewalk while snow drifted in the air around them, enveloping them in wintry lace.

Marc opened the front door and shouted, "Hey Ma, Dad, we're here!"

He turned to Monica and suddenly his eyes changed, became warmer, filled with love. He reached out and touched his finger to the tip of her nose. "You have a snowflake on your nose," he murmured. "Snowflakes only land on people they love," he said. "Lucky you."

"Oh, Marc," she sighed, going into his arms, her face bathed in radiance. "I love you so much."

They were lost in a kiss when someone cleared his throat. Jumping apart, they turned to find Marc's father watching them, amusement gleaming in his eyes, his sandy red hair standing up in tufts on his head, his florid face wreathed in smiles. He was dressed casually and carried a short, squat tumbler of liquor.

Monica smiled to herself. She'd never seen two parents look less like their child than Elliot and Eleanor English. If she didn't know better, she'd think Marc had been mistakenly switched at the hospital.

"We're already starting our toasts," Elliot Walsh English said, holding up the glass and beaming at them. "Happy Thanksgiving."

"Dad," Marc said, whipping off his coat and extending his hand to his father, "this is Monica, but I call her Nicky. Nicky, this is my Dad."

"Mr. English, I'm so happy to meet you."

"No happier than I am to meet you, Nicky," the older man said. "And for heaven's sake, call me Elliot. Come on in here by the fire and get warm." He escorted Monica into the family room where logs blazed cheerily on the brick hearth and two spaniels lazed in front of the fire.

"Monica," Eleanor English said, putting down her knitting and rising from her chair, "how wonderful to see you." She took Monica's hands, a warm smile lighting up her face. After kissing Monica warmly on the cheek, she turned to Marc, opening her arms for his embrace.

"Marc," she whispered, her face filled with love. "Happy Thanksgiving, darling."

"Happy Thanksgiving, Mom." Marc brought a small wrapped box out of his jacket pocket and handed it to her.

"What's this?" his mother asked, beaming with delight.

"A present obviously," Elliot said dryly, his eyes twinkling at Monica. "What can I get you to drink, Nicky? Wine? Brandy? Something mixed?"

"Actually, I'd like a little whiskey, on ice."

"Good!" Elliot rubbed his hands together energetically, then peered over at his wife, whose face was transfixed as she gazed into the small box. "What did you get, Ellie? Something nice?"

"Oh, Marc," she said, lifting her rapt gaze to her son. "Oh, you shouldn't have."

"Now, Ma," Marc said, grinning. "Just put it on. You'll look pretty."

Eleanor lifted a delicate diamond brooch from the box and pinned it to her collar with trembling hands, then kissed her son. "Thank you, Marc. It's so beautiful." She turned to Monica, her eyes warm. "It's lovely, isn't it? He's given me a present every Thanksgiving since he was a little boy."

"It's gotten to be a tradition," Elliot said from the bar. "He started it when we told him—"

"Dad!" Marc said, leaping up from a chair and rushing toward the television. "Is the game on yet?"

"Football?" his mother said, astounded. "You'd watch *football* when you have two lovely women in the room with you?"

Grinning, Marc bent to scratch behind the ears of one of the spaniels. "Hey, football's important to guys."

Eleanor snorted delicately, her eyes laughing. "I told Mr. Hankins to get the toboggan out. If it keeps snowing, I thought you'd like to take Monica out on it."

Marc looked at Monica. "The first snow of the season I used to take out my toboggan, no matter what. That was a ritual."

"Like buying your mother a Thanksgiving present?" Monica asked, smiling.

"Yeah." Marc frowned and stood up, as if he didn't want to talk about the present he'd bought his mother. "Dad, got any beer?"

Elliot chuckled. "Englishes always drink sherry or brandy," he said to Monica, his eyes twinkling. "That's the only way you can tell my boy's—"

"Dad!" Marc interrupted. "That's a terrific jacket. Did you get it at Stackpole's?"

Elliot English looked thoughtfully at his son. "Yes, as a matter of fact, I did." He frowned and looked at Monica, then raised his eyebrows and settled into his favorite chair. Immediately one of the dogs got up and rested its head on his thigh.

Marc sat down next to Monica and put his arms around her. "Nice, huh?" he whispered into her ear.

She nodded, feeling slightly uncomfortable showing affection in front of his parents. She tried to ease away from him but he pulled her closer.

"What's the matter?" he whispered, nibbling at her earlobe. "Embarrassed? Think my parents don't know about kissing and stuff?"

"Marc," Eleanor said, humor edging the warning in her voice. "I don't think Monica's enjoying being teased."

"Yes, she is," Marc said. "You should see her when we're alone. She loves me to tease her."

Monica felt her cheeks turn pink. "Marc," she said under her breath, smiling sweetly but putting daggers into her words, "cut it out."

Marc just laughed and pulled her closer, putting his feet up on the old trunk that served as a coffee table and sliding

lower into the cavernous comfort of the chintz-covered sofa.
"Next year," he murmured. "We'll be in our own home.
We'll have to start our own traditions, Nicky."

Monica couldn't help it. He was incorrigible. She put her
arms around him and hugged him tight, just once, then sat
back and scratched the dog's ear. If dreams could ever come
true, she thought, this would be exactly the kind of life she
would wish for.

Thanksgiving dinner was served in the formal dining
room, where candlelight gleamed against the cherry dining
table and a huge golden turkey sat on a platter next to Elliot's place, waiting to be carved. An arrangement of yel-
low mums and white carnations sat in the center of the table,
which groaned under every conceivable kind of Thanksgiving food.

Wine flowed, a fire crackled in the fireplace and laughter
rang in the air. By the end of the meal, when six different
pies were brought out and displayed on the sideboard,
Monica was more full than she'd been in years, and happier than she'd ever been in her life on a traditional holi-
day.

Eleanor, presumably anticipating that Marc would want
to sit next to Monica, had set two places close together for
them, and now they sat at the end of the meal, happily re-
plete, sipping afterdinner brandy and tea, holding hands and
engaging in desultory conversation with his parents.

"There's only one thing wrong with today," Elliot said,
sitting back and patting his stomach. "There aren't any kids
here. Ellie and I always regretted not having more children,
but—"

"Dad," Marc said quickly, "More brandy?"

Elliot stared at Marc as if astounded at the interruption,
then shook his head, going on with his talk, "We'd tried so
long to have kids that we thought we were much too old—"

"Dad," Marc said, sounding almost frantic, "More coffee? Maybe we could turn on the television and catch part of the game."

"Dammit, Marc, I'm talking," Elliot said in exasperation, then turned again to Monica, smiling. "As I was saying, we were so old, we were afraid to adopt any more kids after getting Marc." He looked expectantly from Monica to Marc. "You two are thinking about getting married and having kids, aren't you?"

Bemused, Monica sat staring at Elliot, then she glanced at Marc, who was looking miserably uncomfortable. "No, Dad," he said. "It's a little early for Nicky and me to discuss kids."

"Well, you come from good hardy stock, Marc," Elliot said, ignoring the tension that had seemed to enter the room. "Your family in Italy produced more kids than they could handle. You sure won't have any trouble producing a few of your own."

Monica stared at Marc, feeling the strangest tingling along her spine. "Italy?" she asked.

Elliot looked startled. "Didn't you know? Marc's adopted. Ellie and I couldn't have children. We got him when we were both in our thirties. That's how the tradition of Marc giving Ellie a present started. We told him when he was about ten years old. It was on a Thanksgiving day, very much like today. We were giving thanks around the table, and we felt it was time for Marc to know. We talked about it, and Marc spoke up at the end of the meal and gave special thanks for having parents who wanted him. The next year, he gave Ellie a present. He's been doing it ever since."

Monica sat staring at Marc, hearing but not quite grasping what had just been said. "Italy?" she said again, her voice so low that only Marc could hear her. Not that it mattered that he'd been born in Italy. It could have been Tim-

buktu. What mattered was that he'd purposely let her
believe he was an English when in fact he wasn't.

She'd chosen Marc to father her child because of his
bloodline, and now she saw that it had been a colossal joke
on her. Marc's genes were probably peasants' genes. But
even that didn't matter. Nothing mattered but that he'd
purposely misled her. He could have told her the first day
she proposed having his child. He *should* have told her. The
point was, he hadn't. The lie of omission didn't make it any
less of a lie.

He took a slow, deep breath and turned his head, meeting her gaze evenly. "Yes. Italy."

She felt something very cold run through her, felt herself
falling into a kind of deep pit, falling faster and faster, farther and farther away from Marc. "You were right then,"
she said lightly, placing her napkin on the table and pushing back her chair. "You don't go to a tanning booth."

She stood up and smiled graciously at Eleanor and Elliot
English, her long years under her parent's tutelage coming
to her aid. "Dinner was lovely," she said sincerely, "but I'm
afraid I have a previous engagement which Marc promised
to take me to. I hope you don't mind our running off like
this."

"Not at all," Elliot said cheerfully, and then the house
was abustle with hugs and kisses as they got their coats and
exchanged goodbyes.

When the front door closed, Monica turned on her heel
and headed blindly for the car, not speaking, walking as if
in a trance. The snow was coming down harder now and was
already almost three inches deep. She picked her way toward Marc's car, her chin up, her expression frozen into
place. She didn't wait for him to open the door, but opened
it and sat down, shutting the door quietly behind her.

When Marc got in the car, she kept her eyes straight
ahead.

"I didn't want you to find out this way," Marc said, staring straight ahead, his face stony.

"You misled me," she said quietly. "You let me believe you were something you're really not."

"Nicky, I thought it would be better to tell you after you realized you loved me."

"Don't call me Nicky," she said coldly, still refusing to look at him. "Take me home, please, then kindly get out of my life."

"Dammit, Monica, I *am* in your life, like it or not," Marc said, turning her to face him.

She stared at him, feeling as cold inside as the snow that swirled around the car. "You should have told me," she said. "The first day in my office, when I told you I wanted you to father my child because you had good genes, you should have told me then."

"Nicky—"

"Don't Nicky me," she shouted, her anger suddenly breaking hot and fiery from beneath the layer of ice that had seemed to surround her. "Don't you see, Marc?" she said, her voice quivering with anger. "You deliberately misled me. How *could* you?"

"Because I love you," he snapped, his voice as angry as hers, his gray eyes filled with fire.

"Not then you didn't," she accused. "You just wanted to sleep with me. You even admitted it. You knew if you'd told me your bloodlines weren't as patrician as I suspected, I'd have thrown you out of my office. And that's why you didn't want to come to your parents' today. You were afraid I'd find out." She turned her head away, feeling tears prick at her eyelids.

"That's right," he said, starting the car and slapping it into gear. "So now you know." He gunned the engine and the tires whined in the snow, then finally gained traction, and the car lurched forward.

Monica sat staring out the side window unseeingly, her hands gripped tightly in her lap. It was all so foolish, really. It didn't matter that Marc was adopted, not now. She loved him. She would have loved him no matter what his lineage. Genes had nothing to do with it any longer.

What mattered was that he'd deliberately misled her. It was as if she'd been standing on firm, solid ground, only to have the rug pulled from beneath her. Nothing was solid anymore, nothing trustworthy. If Marc had lied to her just to get into her bed, would he lie about other things also? More important things? Would he tell her he loved her, for instance, when he really didn't?

She felt a wave of nausea ripple through her and pressed her hand to her mouth. Suddenly, in a blinding flash of clarity, she realized why lies and half-truths were so dangerous. Relationships had to be based on trust. If you couldn't trust the other person, then nothing was reliable.

She suppressed a groan and closed her eyes, resting her head against the car seat, feeling sicker and sicker. Never had her own lies seemed more flagrant. Until now, she had never realized the true import of her own behavior. This is how Andy must have felt. This is how Marc himself would feel if she were to tell him about the skeletons she'd kept hidden in her own closet all these years. Now, more than ever, she saw there was no future with Marc, no future with anyone if she didn't have the courage to share her past.

And the problem was, she couldn't. If she'd reacted this way to Marc's shading of the truth, how would he react to hers? It would be ten times worse, and with good reason. Marc had merely been adopted and not let her know. She had stolen away to Europe, had a baby and given it away for adoption, all without telling the man who'd fathered it, who had already asked her to marry him. She had no excuse except her father's fury, her father's refusal to let her marry Andy and keep the child.

Sickness swept through her as if on a tidal wave. She pressed her lips together and took a deep breath, then let it out slowly. What a mess life was. How totally abysmal the entire process was—the attempts to appear faultless, the schemes to hide one's past mistakes, the shoddy lies, the shabby pretenses. She turned her head to the side and let the tears escape, let them trickle down her face soundlessly, pain expanding inside her in ever-mounting waves.

"Nicky?"

Marc's quiet voice roused her from her despair. She bit her lower lip and surreptitiously wiped away the tears. "Yes?"

"We're home."

She nodded and sat up, keeping her face turned away from Marc, but he wouldn't let her escape. He reached out and fastened a gentle hand on her chin and turned her to face him. "Nicky," he said, his voice filled with his own pain, "I never meant to hurt you. Sometimes it seems I've wanted you forever. When you called me to your office, it was as if God himself had dropped a treasured jewel into my hands.

"I took it, Nicky. I reached right out and grabbed it, and in my colossal pride, I thought I could make you love me. I thought if I could only show you how much I love you, that you'd love me back. Then I'd tell you, when I was sure you loved me for myself, not my blasted genes." He broke off and took a deep breath. "I should have told you right after you went to tea with my mother. I knew then I couldn't keep you away from them any longer, that it was only a matter of time. But I was so scared, Nicky. I was so damned scared. If you had said you'd marry me this morning, I would have told you then, but when you wouldn't . . ."

He groaned softly and let his head drop back. He sat staring at the ceiling of his car, looking utterly depleted, utterly lost. "I don't blame you for feeling the way you do," he said finally. "But—" He raised his head and turned to her, his eyes filled with anguish.

"Nicky, haven't you ever done something you wanted to hide? Haven't you ever made a mistake, done something you were ashamed of? God, Nicky, I'm only human. I admit what I did was wrong. The ends can't ever justify the means, I see that now, but, Nicky *I love you.*"

She felt exquisite pain rise up in her, so sharp, so pointed, she thought for a moment she might die. Nothing in her life had prepared her for this terrible torture. His mistake was so unimportant, so trivial compared to hers, his lie so white when contrasted with the blackness of hers. She wanted to reach out and take him in her arms and hold him, soothe the pain in his face, smooth away the torment. She couldn't bear the thought of what he was feeling, but she could bear the thought of her own fall from grace even less.

He would hate her if she ever told him, utterly despise her, now more than ever. What right had she to react the way she had?

She had to protect herself. Coward that she was, she couldn't bring herself to bare her soul, even if it meant relieving Marc's pain. Revulsion for herself rose up in her, but she fought it.

"I don't want to see you any more, Marc," she said coolly. "Please don't try to call me again."

She opened the door and stepped from the car into the frigid wetness of the snow. Blindly she walked toward her front door. Somehow she got her key in the lock, opened the door, found shelter inside. Then she was stumbling to the lavatory overcome by nausea, at last setting free all the ugliness and pain she'd harbored for so long.

Thirteen

She was pregnant. Beaming, her gynecologist, Dr. Carmody, had confirmed her suspicion, congratulated her, put her on a special diet and set up future appointments.

She was numb. It seemed implausible that there was another life inside her, growing, taking nourishment from her, forming small, invisible organs. She should have been happy, ecstatic even. Instead, she was filled with sick despair. She sat in her office and stared into space, thinking of Marc. She lay in bed at night and stared into the darkness, thinking of Marc. She sat in Dr. Carmody's office and stared at a dog-eared magazine, thinking of Marc.

Visions of Marc haunted her day and night. Not the Marc who'd made exquisite love to her, but that other Marc, the Marc she'd last seen with anguish in his eyes. He loved her, but she hadn't the courage or the grace to love him in return.

"Ms. Bliss?"

Startled, Monica looked up at the nurse who had called her name.

"Dr. Carmody will see you now, Ms. Bliss," the nurse said, smiling.

Monica walked into his office and sat down, over-whelmed by numbness and despair.

"Do you want this baby, Monica?" Dr. Carmody asked, looking at her over his glasses.

She lifted dazed eyes, trying to comprehend the question. Nothing mattered but Marc and that she'd betrayed him—as sure as she'd betrayed Andy so many years ago.

"Monica," Dr. Carmody said. "It's still not too late to terminate this pregnancy. If you're having second thoughts, for heaven's sake consider it. Raising a child by yourself won't be easy. You've obviously realized that, perhaps a little too late, but at least you've realized it."

She stared at him, his words beginning to sink in. "An abortion?" she said, beginning to shake her head, frowning. That's what her father had wanted her to do with her first baby—but she couldn't. Life was a gift from the gods, a miracle formed through the loving embrace of a man and woman.

"I know it is a difficult decision," Dr. Carmody went on, "but a child deserves to be wanted, to have a parent that is genuinely committed."

She stared at him, beginning to feel something in the deepest part of her, where the baby was growing, taking on a life and identity of its own. "No," she said, her eyes fixed directly on his, her mind at peace. "I want this baby."

Dr. Carmody let out a sigh and nodded slowly, thankfully. "Good. Maybe now you'll come out of that mood you've been in the past two weeks and begin to function. There's a life in you, Monica, and it needs you, needs your nourishment and care and concern. I'm convinced—though I don't have any scientific data to uphold my conviction—

but I'm convinced that babies sense their mothers' moods. They know when she's sad or angry or happy. That little thing growing in you these past few weeks has been feeling what you've been feeling, and that's not good. If you want him, Monica, then dammit, you've got to get out of that blue funk you're in and *help* him."

"Help him?"

"Yes! You have to walk and exercise and eat right, but most of all, you have to be happy. Think positive—smile. Make him feel there's a good reason to want to get out of there seven months from now. Bring him out laughing, Monica, not crying or fearful or sad."

Monica felt tears well up in her eyes and she blinked them away. Darn it, it seemed this last month or so all she'd done was cry. Happy tears and sad ones. "It's just I'm so afraid I won't be a good mother, doctor."

"Oh, hell, Monica, there's hardly a woman on the face of the earth who hasn't had that fear, at least with the first baby. Yeah, I know, this isn't your first, but still, it *is* your first—the first you'll keep, bring up on your own." He smiled at her, looking like an affectionate uncle. "You'll do fine, honey."

She took a breath and bit on her lips to keep the tears in check. "I've made so many mistakes in my life, Dr. Carmody. Sometimes I think I'm being selfish to have a baby this way." She closed her eyes. "I know I am."

"Mmm-hmm," he said, beginning to study his fingernails. "So? We all do selfish things, Monica. We all make mistakes. None of us is perfect. What makes you think you should be different from everyone else? Do you think your mistakes are bigger and better than everyone else's?" He snorted derisively. "Hell, Monica, that's pride. That's the sin of pride, to think you're so damned important that you can't be forgiven, can't be redeemed. This baby'll redeem you, one way or the other."

He leaned forward and said sternly, "Stop thinking about yourself so damned much, Monica Bliss, and start thinking about others." He shook his head. "I'm just glad you're having this baby. Maybe you'll find out that mistakes don't count—the only thing that matters is what you do after them. Now get out." He threw his arm out, gesturing at the door. "Get out of here. Don't come back until you're smiling and six more weeks pregnant."

She sat in the chair, feeling her spirits lift for the first time since Thanksgiving Day. "Thank you, doctor," she whispered, smiling, tears misting her eyes. "That means a lot."

He shook his head. "Half of doctoring is sitting here giving advice." He sighed heavily. "Go on! Get out! I got another patient coming in and *she* needs me."

Driving back from the doctor's office, she realized it was the Christmas season. The stores were bedecked with wreaths and ribbons, Christmas lights twinkled in all the windows, trees were festooned with bows and lights, snowmen waved and Santas winked and Rudolphs pranced on rooftops.

She drove to Westfarms Mall and waded into the bustling crowd of shoppers, staring at the children who ran wide-eyed with excitement from toy to toy. Some day, her child would come here, looking at gifts, choosing which toy he or she wanted, shouting and pointing in excitement.

Monica whirled around and hugged herself with joy, letting her eyes travel over the twinkling lights, the angels, the snowmen and Salvation Army Santas ringing bells and singing carols. She dug into her pocketbook and found a wadded-up dollar bill and dropped it in the bucket.

"Thank you, ma'am," the Santa said, beaming. "Merry Christmas!"

"Merry Christmas," she said, a smile wreathing her face.

She strode along, staring into the windows, taking it all in. Christmas carols sounded in the air, bells tinkled, children laughed and cash registers rang and *who* ever said Christmas wasn't wonderful just the way it was? Everyone was always grousing about how the Christmas spirit was gone, that it was too commercial now, but Christmas wasn't something outside, in a store or window display, Christmas was inside, in the heart, in the soul and spirit of man.

Monica came to a thumping halt on the second level of the mall and stared down at the people milling about on the first level, and suddenly she felt something she'd never felt in her life—a great, rising spirit of love. It rose up in her on a golden wave, sweeping away all the pain and disappointment, all the anger at life and herself.

Dr. Carmody's words floated toward her, as sharp and clear as the Christmas air outside. *What makes you think you should be different from everyone else? You think your mistakes should be bigger and better than everyone else's? That's the sin of pride, to think you're so damned important that you can't be forgiven, can't be redeemed.*

She stood on the second level of Westfarms Mall and began to cry, softly, quietly, weeping with joy, having finally discovered the meaning of love.

She went to a nursery and bought the tallest, fattest Christmas tree she could find, then stood and watched as the gnarled old man tied down the trunk of her car, whistling a Christmas carol as he worked.

"Got a nice tree there, ma'am," he said, tipping his hat to her as he stepped back from his work. "You get a friend to untie it and bring it in the house, you hear? It's a heavy one. You won't be able to handle it alone."

"Okay," she promised, smiling, then drove home and asked a neighbor to help her bring in her tree. For the next half hour she waded into the attic, looking for all the tree decorations, the quilted wreaths and Santa Claus mobiles and arrangements that she'd used every year to deck her halls. When they were all gathered in her living room, she poured mulled cider in a pewter cup, put her Christmas albums on the stereo, and began to decorate the tree.

"Next year," she said out loud to the baby inside her, "you'll be doing this with me. Well, maybe not stringing the lights, but you can watch at least."

She would call The Rehab tomorrow. She'd begin working with them to preserve Hartford's historic buildings. Then she'd branch out, she'd become an expert in the legal aspects of historic preservation. Some day she'd travel the country, representing groups and individuals who wanted to preserve parts of the country's history.

And tomorrow she would take the Mary Cassatt painting down from her office wall. She'd give it away to a museum perhaps, or sell it and give the money to an orphanage. One thing was certain—she didn't need it any longer.

She stood back, looking at the lights she'd just put on the tree and realized only one thing was missing. Or rather, one person—Marc.

She sat down heavily and stared at the tree, then put her hand on her stomach. Marc's baby was inside her, and she was talking to it, including it in her life and future plans, yet Marc himself wasn't here.

She sat back and closed her eyes. She had to face it, had to tie up the final strings that would allow her to go forward with her life. He deserved not only her apology, but her truth. If he wanted to hate her, he deserved that too. It was his due. And he deserved to know about the baby, his child.

She sat up and rubbed her forehead. She didn't want to do it, but she knew she must. There were some things you did not for yourself, but for others.

She dialed slowly, then waited, her heart thumping, while his phone rang. She felt a lump form in her throat, and she began to pray he wouldn't be home. Her heart was beating too wildly for her to speak.

"Hello?"

She felt her heart stop, then explode in her breast. "Marc? It's Monica...."

She paced back and forth, back and forth, waiting for him to arrive. She'd put on her black dress and pearls and her highest heels. She'd combed her platinum blond hair until it shone like a ribbon of silk. She'd put blush on her pale cheeks and a touch of pink color on her lips. Taking a deep breath, she tried to calm her heart. It was racing, skipping beats erratically. Her palms were sweaty. She was scared silly.

When the doorbell rang she stopped pacing and stared, her heart throbbing, her stomach churning with apprehension. Slowly she walked to the front door and opened it.

He stood there with his collar turned up against the snow that had begun to fall, his dark hair ruffled by the breeze. "Merry Christmas, Nicky."

She stood there, unable to speak, just looking at him, drinking in the lines at the corners of his eyes, his firm lips, the angle of his nose, the way his hair curled at his collar.

"Merry Christmas, Marc." She stepped back, opening the door wide. "Come in. I hadn't realized it had started to snow."

He shrugged out of his coat and as he turned, she saw a snowflake glittering on his cheek. Melted already, it looked like a teardrop glistening in the lamplight. Hesitantly she reached out and touched it with her fingertip. "You have a snowflake on you," she murmured softly, her eyes filled with love. "Lucky you. Snowflakes only land on people they love."

He looked into her eyes, and his own flared with hope, then he murmured something inarticulate and she was in his arms and they were hugging, holding each other desperately, eyes squeezed shut, bodies pressed together.

"Nicky," he breathed at last. "Oh, Nicky."

She stepped back, her eyes luminous, her face transfigured with both love and sorrow. She touched his face with her hand, rested her palm on his cheek, memorizing the warmth of his skin under hers, drinking in his presence. It was going to be the hardest thing she'd ever done in her life, but she was going to tell him everything. She didn't want to, wished she could put it off forever, but she couldn't. She'd lived with her secret too long, had hidden too much. She needed light and air in her life, and most of all, she needed truth, honesty, facing up to her mistakes rather than trying to hide them.

She took his hand and led him into the living room. "I was decorating the tree," she said, "and I realized something was missing." She turned to face him. "You."

"You said you needed to talk to me."

She nodded and took a calming breath. "Can I get you some mulled cider?"

"Actually, I'd like a beer if you've got one."

"I think there's one left over from when you cooked supper," she said. "I'll see."

In the kitchen, her hands shook as she opened the pop top of the beer can, then she squared her shoulders, patted her stomach and whispered, "Wish your mom good luck," then went out to the living room.

She found Marc beginning to decorate the tree, and something about the happy, domestic scene made her hesitate. Marc would accept her apology along with her decision to marry him. They could spend the next few hours suspended in a loving homecoming, then the weeks would melt into months, and then the baby would be here, and it might be years before she would ever have to tell him.

Or maybe she would never have to. Maybe the past could be effectively buried, put to rest, never to be dredged up or spoken of. Maybe the only truth that was necessary between them had to start today and never include things that had happened to her in another life, another relationship. Some things, perhaps, were better left unsaid.

But then he turned to her and she felt the impact of his gaze all the way through her body, zinging through her like a bolt of lightning. She knew that he was so important, he mattered so much, that he deserved only the finest she could give him—all her truth and all her honesty. He must know her faults as well as her strengths, her failings as well as her triumphs. She must let him decide for himself whether he could love her, not try to trap him with lies and pretense.

She handed him the beer, and said, "Congratulations, Mr. English, you're going to be a daddy."

"Oh, god," he said wonderingly. "Really?"

She nodded, tears misting her eyes. "Mmm-hmm. Dr. Carmody made it official a couple weeks ago."

"And you waited this long to tell me?"

He looked excited and angry at the same time, and she realized that she would have to get used to people being angry at her. If she made mistakes, she would have to take the consequences. That's what being an adult was all about.

"At first, I was in shock," she explained. "For a while, that whole mess on Thanksgiving overshadowed everything. I couldn't think about the baby because I was so busy regretting how I'd treated you."

"Oh, Nicky," he said, reaching out to press his hand against her stomach. "Nicky, honey."

She came close to him. "You can't feel it yet. It's still too small."

"Can we make love?"

"Yes," she murmured, her eyes filled with love and sorrow.

"Do you want to?"

She wanted to more than anything, but she knew she had to talk first. "Later I do. If you'll still want to after we talk."

"I want to now," he said, his voice low and filled with urgency. He slid his hand down between her legs and slowly pulled up her dress. She sank against him, going weak with longing, trying to fight the waves of desire that spread through her like wildfire. "Oh, Nicky," he breathed, caressing her with urgent fingers, "You feel so good."

She tried to fight the urge to respond, but her body wouldn't let her. When he searched for her mouth, she responded ardently, kissing him feverishly and running her hands into his hair.

"Are you sure it's all right?" he asked breathlessly as he lay down with her on the floor. "Are you sure we won't hurt the baby?"

"It's all right," she breathed, tugging at his shirt, then sucked in her breath as he entered her and let it out on a long, ragged moan of pleasure.

Inarticulate gasps escaped her. It had never been this good before, never this erotic. She wrapped her legs around his waist, lifting her hips so that he thrust into her with his entire length. She felt him with exquisite awareness, as he thrust and withdrew, each time reaching farther and farther into her soul.

Pleasure cascaded over her, rippled through her, pulled her down into its fine, dark chasm. She was music, and she was light. She was joy and she was beauty. She was on fire, sinking into ecstasy, dancing with rapture. Slowly, rapidly, without time and with no limits, she circled and circled toward the center of the universe, falling and crying, laughing and gasping at the incredible beauty that filled her, soared inside her, emancipated her.

"I love you," she whispered, over and over, until she felt the wave crash over her in splendor, shattering the world in a blinding flash of glory.

Holding him to her, she cried his name.

"I didn't mean for this to happen," she said to him later, lying in his arms, looking into his eyes.

"I did."

She smiled slowly, shaking her head at his willfulness. Then she sobered. "When I found out that you were adopted, the first thing I thought was that you didn't tell me because you just wanted to sleep with me. I was afraid it was just sex for you."

He shook his head. "I admit I love to sleep with you. I've never felt this kind of pleasure before. But that's not all it is, not by a long shot. I love you, Monica. It's natural that because I love you, I want to make love with you. My body fits with yours. It's made for yours. But that's not the only reason I want you."

She sat up and began to dress. "I need to talk with you, Marc," she said slowly. "There are things you don't know about me, things that might change how you feel."

"Oh?" He zipped up his trousers and buttoned his shirt, looking abstracted. "Why tell me, then?"

"Because I love you. Because I want you to love me for me, not for the image I've projected." She rubbed the bridge of her nose, feeling an aching throb beginning far back in her head. "You say you love me, but you don't really know me. You don't know anything about me, about what I've been and what I've done."

She went to stand at the window, watching the snow whip across the yard, propelled by high winds that bent the trees forward and rattled the windows. It looked as if they were in for a blizzard. Shivering, she rubbed her arms and began to speak.

"At Thanksgiving, when I found out that you were adopted, at first I was shocked, because of course I had no idea. But very quickly, my shock changed to something else, and I realized that what I was feeling was what Andy Emerson had felt a long time ago, after the summer I went to Europe.

"I've always regretted what I did that summer, but I'd never experienced anything like it from the other side. I'd never loved someone and then found out they'd done something that undermined my trust."

She turned and saw that Marc was sitting on the couch, his hands in his trouser pockets, slouched down and watching her, his face unreadable. She rubbed her arms again, as if to ward off a chill, and wandered toward the fireplace. She came to a stop in front of Amy's picture. Slowly, she reached out and picked it up.

"This isn't my cousin's little girl," she said, turning to Marc and extending the photograph to him. "She's mine."

It felt as if a year was passing, but slowly Marc took a hand out of his pocket and took the photograph. "Yours?" he said. His voice was curiously neutral, as if he weren't in the least surprised.

She swallowed awkwardly and nodded. "Andy's and mine. I got pregnant my sophomore year of college, but I didn't realize it until I came home. My father sent me to Dr. Carmody, and a couple days later he got the report that I was pregnant."

She looked into the past, remembering that day as if it were yesterday. She'd been called into the den, the same room where her mother had always sat every afternoon, drinking. "Well," her father said, his face as remote and cold as a gravestone. "You're pregnant, Monica Marie. Would you care to explain how it happened?"

She sat down so quickly it was more like she collapsed. Her face went white and she felt faint. She'd suspected, but had refused to believe it. Now she felt anger sizzle through her. She tossed her head back and crossed her legs languidly. "How do you think it happened, Father?" she asked sarcastically.

"You've been sleeping with Andy Emerson, I presume."

"Correct."

He had leaned forward, and for the first time in her life, she saw his veneer crack and his face fill with high red color. "I give you the best of everything and you throw it in my face."

"You haven't given me anything," she cried. "You've given me plenty of beautiful things—but nothing that really matters." She threw her arm out to indicate their surroundings. "What possible good did all this do? It didn't make Mama happy. It didn't stop her from killing herself with expensive booze."

Jason Bliss sat back, suddenly looking tired and old. "In a few years you'll be going to law school. You're on the brink of a wonderful life, Monica. I won't have you ruin it for a boy who doesn't have half the brains you do, who'll never amount to anything."

"I *love* him!" she cried, sitting forward, her own face wrought with emotion.

He propped his elbow on the arm of his chair and wiped his brow, then sat staring at the cold fireplace. "I've arranged for an abortion. There's a clean clinic in Mexico. You'll fly there this weekend. Thank God we caught it early enough."

"An abortion?" She stared at her father. She both loved him and hated him, and didn't know which emotion was stronger. "I can't," she whispered. "I can't."

He'd looked up then, his face twisted with some feeling she couldn't understand. "It won't hurt, honey. I promise."

She shook her head, tears glistening in her eyes. "No, Daddy, it's not *me*, it's my baby." She'd begun to sob. "Please, Daddy. Please don't make me do that."

He'd held her then, the only time in her life she was ever held by her father. Finally he'd agreed to send her away to have the child. "I have clients who've been trying to adopt. We can arrange for them to take it. Then you'll come right home and finish school. Is that clear, Monica Marie?"

Monica stared into the past, remembering it all, seeing for the first time something she'd never seen before. She recognized that look on her father's face—it was pain for her, not for himself. She turned slowly toward Marc, her face filled with incredulity. "He *did* love me," she said. "You were right. In his own way, I believe he did."

She didn't know when it had happened, but Marc was with her, holding her, nodding, his face filled with sadness. She swallowed awkwardly and met his gaze. "I didn't tell Andy, Marc. Daddy wouldn't let me. I went to Europe and had the baby and the Alversons, Daddy's clients, took Amy that very day." She looked at the photograph Marc had set on the mantel. "They send me pictures of her every once in a while. She's sixteen now. They moved away after they adopted her.

"When Andy found out, he hated me. He hated what I'd done—but not as much as I hated myself. I was weak and spineless, but I pushed it all out of my mind in college and then in law school. I put everything I had into school and the day I graduated with highest honors, Daddy brought me to his firm and showed me the office that would be mine. That's when he gave me the Mary Cassatt painting. He told me it was to make up for giving up Amy."

Tears sprang into her eyes, but she kept on talking because she had to get it all out. "Oh, Marc," she whispered, closing her eyes against the pain, "I saw my father for what he was that day, and saw myself—I felt I was as bad as he was. I hate that painting, but I've kept it as a kind of penance, so I'd never forget."

"Or ever forgive," Marc said quietly.

She looked at him, puzzled. "What do you mean?"

"You've hated your father long enough, Monica. And you've punished yourself enough, as well. Do you really think what happened was wrong? Your dad was a product of his generation. Well-brought-up girls didn't have children out of wedlock. The only trouble is, they did, just as they do today. What your father tried to do was save you from marrying under the gun. That's a rough way to begin any marriage, Nicky, and even though his methods were deplorable, I have a hunch his motives were pure. And lots of girls have given up babies, Nicky. My mother did."

She stared at him, feeling a lifting in her heart, a soaring of her spirit. He was telling her he understood. He was telling her she was all right. It was not comdemnation he gave her, but forgiveness. "Your mother?" she asked softly.

"As my father mentioned, I came from a family in Italy. My mother got pregnant the way you did, and she had her baby, who turned out to be me. She gave me up, and I was raised by the two most loving people in the world. I've been grateful to my real mother and my adopted one all my life, ever since I found out. Some day, Amy will be grateful, too."

"Then you don't think I'm horrible?"

He reached out and smoothed his hand across her face. "I love you, Nicky. I've told you that a few dozen times in the past. I told you that earlier today. I'm telling you that now."

She went into his arms, pressed herself against him, hugging him with all the strength she had, her eyes filling with tears. "Damn," she said, her voice husky with emotion, "I've cried more in the past month than I've ever cried in my life. Tears of sorrow, tears of joy."

"Which are these?" Marc asked gently.

"Joy," she whispered, lifting her face to his. "Incredible, wonderful joy."

She drank him in, feasted her eyes on his beloved face, sank into the redemption he offered her. "Oh, Marc, you can't know what this means to me. I feel whole again, free for the first time in sixteen years. I'm going to have your baby, and I'm going to have you. I'm afraid to believe it, afraid to trust it. It's as if you'll go away tonight and come to realize you really hate me, that you couldn't love a woman who's made the mistakes I've made."

Marc sighed and drew her into his embrace, resting his chin atop her head. "You know, I figured you might think this way. That's why I've got something here you might be interested in." He drew a piece of paper from his breast pocket and held it out to her.

Puzzled, she took it from him and opened it, then stared in amazement. It was a copy of Amy's birth certificate. She lifted stunned eyes. "You knew?"

He nodded. "For a while now. After we came back from Vermont, I had one of the detectives I know nose around a little into your past. I told him you went to Europe, so he took a weekend jaunt to track down what you did there. It wasn't difficult, Monica."

"But that means you've known—"

"Since before Thanksgiving."

She stared at him, the full import of his words sinking in. "Then you knew all about it when you asked if I hadn't ever done something I was ashamed of."

He nodded. "I hoped you'd tell me then, Nicky. When you didn't, my heart broke, but I decided I'd give you till Christmas. If you hadn't called by then, I was going to come here and force the issue in the open. I figured that's what this all had to be about—your fear of getting involved with me, for fear I'd try to take away the baby. The way you worded the legal document you drew up for me to sign gave me a clue. You stated specifically that no information discovered about your past could be used in any way against you to take away the child."

"I added that just before we went to Vermont," she said, still stunned. "I guess I wasn't thinking clearly. I was so afraid I'd end up making love with you. After the night when you made dinner, I knew I couldn't resist you much longer, and I was so scared, Marc. I thought if you ever found out about me you'd hate me, and think I'd be an unfit mother."

"Nicky, I tried for years to go out with you, but you always snubbed me. Then two years ago, you agreed to go out and I made the biggest blunder of my life. I thought the no-nonsense approach might work with a business-minded woman like you, so I came right out and said I wanted to sleep with you. It was the stupidest thing I've ever done, and I deserved the black eye you gave me.

"Then you called me and asked me to come to your office. I hadn't the foggiest idea what you wanted to see me about, but I presumed it would be business. When you told me what you wanted, I felt as if I'd died and landed in heaven. There you were, looking as delicious as a ripe plum, and you were falling right into my hands.

"That's why I did what I did, why I didn't tell you I was adopted. Fair means or foul, I meant to get you this time. And I would have, even if you hadn't been able to bring yourself to tell me. But honey, I'm so glad you did. It means more to me than you can ever know. It means you trust me, that you really care for me."

"Care for you?" she said softly, her eyes filled with love. "I love you, Marc English. Somehow I must have known you were the man for me when I called you. I wouldn't admit it, but I wanted your baby because of *you*, not your silly genes. You could be a Martian and it wouldn't matter. I love you, more than I ever thought it was possible to love any man."

He grew serious. "More than Andy Emerson?"

She nodded, her certainty clear in her direct, unyielding gaze. "I was a girl then, loving a boy. I'm a woman now, loving a man, the finest man I've ever had the honor to know. And if that proposal for marriage is still open . . ."

He drew her into his loving embrace. "Actually I was kind of hoping we could have a little more courting time. I've grown accustomed to the chase, but seeing as we've got a little English sprouting, I guess we better find us a preacher."

"Do you mind that I'm pregnant so soon?" she asked anxiously.

"Mind? The sooner we start our family, the better. I'm getting old, Nicky. I *need* to have kids real soon, while I can still enjoy them."

"You'll never be too old," she said, laughing. "You taught me how to laugh, how to loosen up, even how to cry." She shook her head at the man she loved. "Oh, Marc English, you're a helluva guy."

"What'll we name him?" Marc asked suddenly.

"Him?"

"Yeah, I kinda like the idea of a son first."

"Marc, Jr.?"

He thought about it, then said slowly, "I was thinking more along the lines of Jason, after your father, and if it's a girl, Angela after your mother."

"Oh, Marc," she murmured, feeling this gesture of his love for her seep deeply into her bones. "I have never been happier."

"You will be, Nicky," he said, smiling tenderly. "I'll make sure of it. Me and the kids—we'll dedicate our lives to making you happy."

She went into his embrace, radiant with love, knowing that she had found what she'd never thought possible, the true and lasting love of a wonderful man, a love based on mutual truth and trust, a love that would endure forever.

Deep in the womb, curled together in preconscious slumber, Angela and Jason English stretched in silent contentment, their tiny hearts pumping strongly, their bodies forming, strong and straight and proud. And it was overwhelmingly clear, even to the most impartial observer, that they were going to be the most beautiful twins in the world.

*   *   *   *   *

 *Silhouette Desire*

COMING NEXT MONTH

#415 FEVER—Elizabeth Lowell
World traveler Lisa Johansen had never met a man like Ryan McCall before. Their love grew in a sweet summer meadow, but would the bond between them be broken when Rye revealed his true identity?

#416 FOR LOVE ALONE—Lucy Gordon
His new bride woke, remembering nothing, and Corrado Bennoni was glad. Fate had given him a second chance to win Philippa...for love alone.

#417 UNDER COVER—Donna Carlisle
Detective Teale Saunders saw an innate honesty beneath con man David Carey's polished facade. When she fell in love with the man she was duty-bound to arrest, she learned that things aren't always black or white.

#418 NO TURNING BACK—Christine Rimmer
Jake Strand had seen her at the worst of times, and Caitlin O'Neill wanted no part of him. But for Jake she had been his turning point, and his hope for the future lay with her.

#419 THE SECOND MR. SULLIVAN—Elaine Camp
Notorious Beau Sullivan wasn't at all like Kelly had expected—and when he started to romance her, she found her ex-brother-in-law hard to resist!

#420 ENAMORED—Diana Palmer
Neither Melissa Sterling nor Diego Laremos was able to resist their passion in the steamy Guatemalan jungle. Torn apart by their families' past, they had to learn trust before they could be reunited.

Silhouette Intimate Moments

THIS MONTH
CHECK IN TO
DODD MEMORIAL HOSPITAL!

Not feeling sick, you say? That's all right, because Dodd Memorial isn't your average hospital. At Dodd Memorial you don't need to be a patient—or even a doctor yourself!—to examine the private lives of the doctors and nurses who spend as much time healing broken hearts as they do healing broken bones.

In UNDER SUSPICION (Intimate Moments #229) intern Allison Schuyler and Chief Resident Cruz Gallego strike sparks from the moment they meet, but they end up with a lot more than love on their minds when someone starts stealing drugs—and Allison becomes the main suspect.

In May look for AFTER MIDNIGHT (Intimate Moments #237) and finish the trilogy in July with HEARTBEATS (Intimate Moments #245).

Author Lucy Hamilton is a former medical librarian whose husband is a doctor. Let her check you in to Dodd Memorial—you won't want to check out!

IM229-1R